I0543322

Richard

BLOOD BROTHERHOOD BOOK 5

KATHI S. BARTON

This is a work of fiction. Names, characters, places, and incidents are products of the author's imagination or are used fictitiously and are not to be construed as real. Any resemblance to actual events, locations, organizations, or persons, living or dead, is entirely coincidental.

World Castle Publishing, LLC
Pensacola, Florida
Copyright © Kathi S. Barton
Paperback ISBN: 9781629894973
eBook ISBN: 9781629894980
First Edition World Castle Publishing, LLC, July 11, 2016
http://www.worldcastlepublishing.com
Licensing Notes
All rights reserved. No part of this book may be used or reproduced in any manner whatsoever without written permission, except in the case of brief quotations embodied in articles and reviews.
Cover: Karen Fuller
Editor: Eric Johnston
Editor: Maxine Bringenberg

Richard

PROLOGUE
1816

"You will go to the home, and you will kill them both. If I so much as get wind that either of them live, I will hunt you and your family down and kill them all, making you watch as I do so." The faerie before her nodded, his wings moving so quickly that he appeared to be floating in the air without aid. Lucia knocked him out of the air and wanted to ask him to repeat what she'd said to him, but he just lay before her, his face nearly buried in the dirt. "What are you waiting for? Do you think I should go and hold them for you whilst you remove their heads? Or perhaps you wish for me to drive the wood into their chests and reward you for my work?"

"Nay, my lady. Both of them will die this day. This I promise you." She waited for him to leave her, but he lay there. Before she could ask him what he was waiting for, he lifted his head to glance at her. "He is said to be very powerful, my lady. Much stronger than even I am, being a lowly faerie and all. All I have to help me in this task is my magic, puny

5

as it is."

"You are asking for something? Perhaps you think you should have some of what I have?" He told her no and whimpered when she stood up. "You have it in your head to go there, to have some of me within yourself to kill this man? You wish a part of my magic? Do you think he will not know, should you fail, that it was me? That he will not smell me upon you?"

"Nay, my lady. I was thinking that you could give me a weapon to use. A sword to defend myself should he arise whilst I'm there." She'd not thought of that, giving him a weapon. But there wasn't any reason he should know that. "I should like to be able to come back here and report that I have done as you asked. I fear that should I only be able to kill one of them first, it will be doubly hard to kill the other with my magic drained so much."

"There are ample things for you to take with you at the door. I am not stupid enough to think you could do this without my help. But bring them back to me if you please. I have a fondness for those things." There wasn't anything there, and when he returned to her to ask after them, she blamed it on someone else. Anyone but herself.

After he left her the second time, she sat in her chair. It was nothing more than a simple chair, not even made wholly of wood, but it served. For now. Someday, soon she hoped, she'd get her something worth sitting in. But for now she would use some of her magic, very little of it, to make it appear that it was as grand as she was.

A knock at her door had her tensing up. Surely he could not have done what she'd asked so soon. But when the Council of Magic and the Gathering entered her chambers, Lucia had a fear so deep that she felt her magic curl around her. When they both visited a person—both the ones that made the rules and those that punished when rules were not followed—you knew that something was wrong.

"Lucia Alvarez, it has been brought to our attention that you have been using magic to better your own station in life. Using it in ways that are against the rules of our kind. Of all kinds, as a matter of fact." She wanted to point out that bettering her own station in life should always come first, but he continued before she could. Probably a good thing when she thought on it. "And as such, after looking into the matter, we have deemed the accusation to be true. You have murdered others for their magic, lesser beings that would have added nothing to your own base. You've stolen from higher faeries; not just their magic, but things that you have used to make yourself richer and your magic darker. You have also not paid your dues to us, something that you were to do every year on the day of your birth. These rules, and a great many others that you have dismissed for some reason, are to be followed to the letter, and this you know. You will come with us, and be heard before the Gathering."

It was on the tip of her tongue to tell them to go away. That she had more important things going on right now that didn't have anything to do with them. Of course, that would be a mistake. One thing that she had learned over the decades she'd been alive was that she wasn't to mess with the Council. And never ever the Gathering, which was known to be harsh in their judgment, as well as quick.

She found herself transported before the Gathering and her hands bound in magic so that she couldn't use her magic against them. It thrilled her to no end that they were afraid of her. But when they began to speak, each of them naming a law she had broken or a deed that she had done against humans and her kind, she knew that someone had turned her in. Someone who was going to be dead, and very soon.

When the list seemed to be coming to an end, Lucia wasn't sure if she was supposed to be excited that her list of grievances was so long or pretend that she was saddened by it. Either way, she was pretty sure that she was in trouble. When asked what she had to say about her list of crimes, she pouted prettily at them.

"I don't know what you're speaking of. I have been a model faerie. I have.... As you might not know, I have been a volunteer at the local branches of the hospital, as well as working in other places that I cannot name at the moment." There weren't any places that she'd been working, nor had she ever volunteered. It was Ryiah who had done all of this and put her name to it, so if questioned, she would look like she had. "I have several letters of acclaim that tells of my work at the hospital. I am also on the board of directors at the library." She tried to think what else was on that list, but came up blank. "This was all just a mistake," she told them. "Whoever has turned me in for these crimes, they must have some sort of grudge against me."

"Can you produce these letters?" She nodded and snapped her fingers. Nothing happened, of course, but she asked them for this one bit of magic to do as they asked. She needed to return to her home to get them and to bring them back to them. Just as soon as she was finished with the project she was working on. "No, that won't be necessary. We shall send someone to your home to retrieve them. Where do you have them filed?"

Again, Lucia had no idea. There had been a list on her desk, but where was it now? She wasn't sure where she'd put the paperwork that had been given to her over the last few months. She was positive that she'd not tossed it away, but she'd not filed it either. Instead of telling them this, she asked to have her assistant brought to them so that she could go with them. In seconds, less really, Ryiah was standing by the dais with the Gathering.

Ryiah wasn't happy…that much was obvious. But Lucia didn't care what she was upset about now. It was more than likely something that she'd done, but so long as Ryiah did as she was told when she was told to do it, she could be as pissed as she wanted.

After the Gathering told her what they needed, Ryiah glared at her. It would have been her greatest pleasure to kill her. Every second of every day she wished the woman dead. But she couldn't kill her. Few knew the reason why, but Lucia wasn't able to even prick Ryiah's fingers without great pain to herself. But that didn't stop her from making her the scapegoat of every one of her deeds. Or at the very least the one that got her out of trouble.

The paperwork was brought to the Gathering, and once it was verified that it was real, Lucia was sent to a cell. It was better than having her head removed any day, but she didn't want to be here at all. The next ten days, very little in the long run, was to be her punishment. It would keep her from her tasks and information. Information that she needed.

But alas, she would do her time for now, because it was better than the alternative. This was nothing, not for the deaths of the hordes of people that she had murdered. Not for the beheading of several heads of their government. She was in this cell for ten days because she had not reported the fact that she was now living in a nest of vampires. Who, she might have pointed out to them—but didn't—were all dead. Also by her hand.

Ryiah came to see her on the last day of her sentence. She'd been calling to her since she'd been locked up, but today was the first time she showed. There was and would always be bad blood between these two, but to leave her without one bit of information, or even a few new clothes to put on, was cruel. And Lucia knew her sister was about as cruel as it came when she needed something from her.

"I'm only here to inform you that I have moved my things to the family home. I will no longer work for you." Lucia only smiled at her. "You have no hold over me. I owe you nothing. And should you try and kill me, as you have done to so many others that I cannot fathom why you've not been killed by the Gathering, know that I have a list of not only where you have put the bodies, but also magic that can be used to watch you do the deeds."

"I don't care what you think you have over me, Ryiah. You're nothing, and will never be anything more than a pawn in my plans. So you will move your things back to the house where I am. I have more need of you than before. The Council will keep a closer eye on me and my magic now, and I have no desire to be brought here again. And since you have decided, for whatever reasons that you have in that small mind of yours, to not come here when I call to you, I will punish you. Not as badly as I would like, but you will suffer." Ryiah told her that she didn't care. "Oh, but you should, Ryiah. You really should. Being my sister will not only open doors for you, it can shut them as well. When the Council finds out that you have lied to them to save me, what do you think they'll do to you?"

"No more than you have tried over the centuries, Lucia. In fact, I think death would be better than living with you for the rest of my days." Lucia stood up and came to the bars to scare her sister. But Ryiah held her ground, even went so far as to lift her chin in an act of defiance. "I despise you, Lucia. I truly do."

"I care not for your feelings, Ryiah. Should it be possible, I would gladly kill you myself. But our blood relationship prevents it." Ryiah just stood there, and Lucia wouldn't have believed it possible, but she hated her sister even more in that moment because she truly looked as if she did not care what Lucia did to her. "You'll do as I say because you know the consequences should you not. I own you. And will until I say differently."

Ryiah didn't move. Didn't so much as blink at her. Lucia was fearful of her sister, if the truth was known. No one but her knew Ryiah for what she was...a powerful faerie in her own right. But Lucia had always made sure that she was close by to control it. And if Ryiah ever found her mate, then Lucia would pay, and pay dearly.

"I loathe you, Lucia." Lucia smiled. She'd won. Again. And after waiting for her to tell her she was moving back, Lucia said nothing. So apparently she was going to be denied her begging, a pleasure that she tried to get from her sister as much as she could. "The woman is dead. The man you tried to have murdered? He is alive, but saddened because of you. And I do hope you know that when the other comes to claim you as his mate, you will no longer have a hold over me. A mate to you means my freedom. I'm going to do everything in my power to make sure that he finds you, too."

"You will die when he finds me. I will make sure that I'm there when your head is removed from your body. No one will be there to save you, least of all me." Ryiah said nothing, but did smile. A frightening sort of not giving a crap sort of smile. "Or perhaps I will bind you to him, to be his sex slave

11

whilst I have my fun."

"I will have no ties to him but through your magic. I will murder him before he even touches me." She could do that, Lucia thought. Murder a man that was nothing to her. "Think well on your next move, Lucia. I will be your downfall if you make me move back to your home."

Of course, she had to live with her. How else was she to keep an eye on her sister? Keep her away from all men that she did not deem to be safe and not her mate? Ryiah wasn't going anywhere, and if she had to make her hurt to stay, then she would. Murdering her would be better, but again she wasn't able to do that. At least not by her own hand. And she wasn't worried about her having a mate. Lucia had taken precautions on that score, and he would soon be dead too. Or he'd better be. But Ryiah would not know that.

"I care not what you think you will or won't do to me, Ryiah. I am your master and I will expect you there when I return." She sat on the bed and glared at her sister. "Malcomb will be my mate, but not for many, many decades if he lives through this. I hope that he ends his own life. It will save me so much trouble. But if he does not by then, I have a plan that will make you heel, much better than you are now. Go to the house, have it cleaned from top to bottom. Then I want six... nay, seven men in my bed awaiting me. They will fuck me until I am sated. Then I will deal with you."

After she left, Lucia sat there thinking. If her sister ever found out, ever even had an idea what she'd done to her, Lucia would be dead, by Ryiah's hand. In this, her death would be justified. The bond that held them safe from each other would be broken, and her sister would be well within her rights to murder her. No harm to one that is blood. The rule, like so many others, had been one of the first ones that she'd broken.

And there would be little that Lucia could do to stop her.

"So long as she never finds her mate, I will be safe." It was her only fear…to be found out by Ryiah when she came into her power with her other half. Her magic, the very part of her that Lucia had stolen from her, would come to her sister then, and Lucia would be left with nothing. Not one single bit of magic to even call her sister to her. "Her magic is safe for me, and I will never let her go to find him. Whoever he might be."

~~~

Rick moved among the ruins of his brother's home. The pain in his own body was only secondary to the one in his heart. His wounds would heal when he next fed. He knew this, but the death of one that he loved as much as he did his brother would haunt him for the rest of his life. The death of his sister-in-law hurt them all.

Rick had been staying with his brother and his family last night or he might not have been able to pull his brother from the burning shell. He had no idea if a stray ember from the fires from the night before had started the blaze, or if someone had dropped a candle. As it was, his brother's lovely wife had been killed by a stake through the heart, more than likely from falling timber, before he could get to her. Rick didn't know why; if it was set, who would do this to his brother and his wife? But he was going to find out.

Turning when someone said his name, he looked at his only friend.

"You must go to ground, my friend. Should you stay out here longer, you will join your sister-in-law in the afterlife, and she will be most upset with you should you not avenge her death." Janell looked around, then back at him. "I will find she who has done this. And when I do, I will make sure that she suffers greatly for it."

"You know that it was set then?" She nodded at him. "Then I have no wish for you to get into trouble either. Nay, do not do this for me. I shall take care of it. Besides, you know as well as I that it was Lucia." Janell said nothing, not even to acknowledge what they both knew. "She meant to destroy him for a reason that I cannot know."

"It is said that Mary was to die in childbirth and Lucia was to be Malcomb's second mate. I do know that the earth says this, but I cannot believe that such a match would have been correct. Your brother is a good man, kind and full of life. While Lucia is —"

"She's a bitch and a murderer. And should she find out that I am the one that turned her in for her crimes all those weeks ago, I will be next on her list. I don't even know why she bothered with poor Malcomb. He leads such a quiet life, not even bothering to be involved in family much. He is so timid and afraid of things." Janell smiled at him. "You find this funny?"

"Nay, my lord, I do not. But she is with the Council as we speak. She sits in a cell awaiting her fate. The Council has found her guilty of the charge and she will be punished. I know not which charge, but it is said to have her behind bars until such time as things can be carried out." He asked her how long that would be. "I do not know that either, my lord. The Council has their own rules and secrets, and my kind, or any kind of being, is not privy to them. I only know that she was taken before them and that she was found guilty."

Rick felt somewhat better, even relieved, but his brother and his family had suffered at her hands and he wanted revenge. But it had been taken out of his hands now. She would die quickly and not suffer in ways that he was...or his brother.

When he felt something akin to a blade into his heart, he fell to his knees. He knew what it was immediately. Malcomb was no more.

"My lord?" He waved Janell away, his heart tearing apart, because as surely as he was standing here, he knew that his brother had met the sun. His pain for the death of his wife was just too much. "My lord, you're frightening me. Come away from there and tell me...." When she paused, he knew that she was as aware, if not more so, of what happened as he was.

"He's dead." Janell put her arms around him and helped him to an area in the yard that had not been a part of the devastation. "Malcomb hurt terribly. Even when I tried to help him out of the burning house, he begged me to leave him behind. Now...now he is gone from me."

"It is the way of your kind." He sat there thinking of his kind. The way that they took mates to make them stronger, yet it killed a part of them when their mates were gone. "Your own mate, she is coming too. Her love will mend you. I know this."

"I've no wish to meet her." Janell said nothing. "What should happen to her? When I cannot care for her the way that I did my brother?"

"I cannot tell you of that future. You know this. I only know that she comes to you. That is more than you should know of this." He did know it, but it wasn't something that he liked. "I have given you a part of me, my lord. You can now be in the sunlight because of our bond. This will keep you safe. And once you have taken your bride, she too will enjoy the benefits that come with you being her other half."

As he sat there, Janell fussing with him about what he was doing, he looked down and saw the faerie garden that he had sat on. When he looked at her, he could see her shock and tried to stand up to move. He felt the pain almost as soon as he opened his mouth to ask her where he was, on whose garden he had lain.

His back and neck burned as if someone was setting hot stones to his skin. Even as he cried out that he wanted help with it, he knew that Janell couldn't help him. Wouldn't be able to, because she knew, just as he did, what was happening to him. Someone was killing him.

As he cried out over and over with the pain of it, he saw the blood as it ran down his body and covered his chest and arms, as whatever was going on with his body was diminishing. When it was over, the pain was less and he could feel that whatever had happened had created a marking on his body that would never leave him.

"She is a great and powerful being, the woman you have brought awake." He looked up, seeing Janell bowing before a being that was as pure white as his blood was red. "You must stand and thank her, my lord. She has given you a great gift."

"I hurt too badly for me to consider this a gift." The laughter had him looking up again. He felt himself being pulled to the woman—for he had no doubt that was what the being was—his feet not touching the ground that neither of them stood upon, his pain gone. "Thank you, my lady. But since I think you hurt me, I think you owe me as well."

"I have given you all that I can, Lord Richard James." He felt his heart pound in his chest and wondered at it. "You will face many things in your life. A great many deaths yet, some that will bring you yet again to your knees. But know that as you stand before me, you will survive. Nothing will kill you."

"The sun, it cannot, but a sword can remove my head." She told him no longer. "I am but a mere vampire, my lady. Subject to the ways of my kind."

"I have chosen you, with the help of your friend here, to help me with a great project. It will be many years from now. Decades will pass…centuries before she comes to you." He asked her who. "A being so strong that she will give you more than you have ever seen. A power that will dominate all that bow before you. And a love that will know no bounds. A love that will last you both until the end of all time."

"I'm not deserving. I think you…perhaps you meant my brother, Malcomb. He was a man to deserve such a gift. Not I." She smiled at him and turned to look at Janell. It was then that he saw the jagged scar on the woman's face. It marred her from hairline to chin. "Who would dare do such a thing to you?"

"It is of no consequence now that I have found you, Lord James. She will suffer greatly for hurting me thusly. When you meet a woman of great humility, you will save her for me. She will give you her heart, but not easily. Her body will be the greatest gift that a man can receive. Yet before she comes, there will be much death; you will witness many lives being taken in the name of greed. This woman and those that you are with will gain all that I have given you this day."

He closed his eyes when she asked him to. When he opened them again Rick could see it then, markings all around his neck and down his back. He knew that magic had put them there. Because of what he was, there should have been no magic to mark him so. Magic, very strong and powerful magic, had done what nothing else could. He looked at her when she said his name.

"What is this?" She only smiled at him. "You've marked me as belonging to you. What if I…? What would you do should I try and end my life?"

The sword was in her hand before he could blink. She

swung it around, cutting into his throat as soon as she lifted it to her shoulder. He felt it slice through him. Grabbing his neck to try and stop the flow of blood or his head from falling, he felt nothing. Not a drop of his blood, nor even a small tear to his flesh. And there was no pain. He asked her if she'd missed.

"Nay, I do not miss when I wield the sword of my kind." Again, he asked her what she was. "You will live as I have decreed. And this favor I ask of you, you will carry it out for me and things will...the earth and the inhabitants of it will thank you for it."

"Why me?" She only smiled at him again. Rick had a feeling that even if he were to ask her a million times, he'd not get an answer from her. "My lady, I just want to live my life as a vampire. I have no desire to find a mate. I don't want anyone in my life that.... Well, I should like to join my brother. And there is a woman who will wish me dead soon enough. I would rather not subject a mate to such—"

"The matter is closed." He felt his anger take him, burn over him like acid. But when she laughed, he knew a new kind of pain, consuming him in ways that had him thinking the marking of his body had been mere child's play, his body stiff with it. "'Twill do you not one bit of good to try and harm me, Lord Richard James. Should you try, even thinking that I will end this between us, it will not work. You belong to me. And until you have completed this favor, you will be alive and healthy no matter what things come your way. Even during what you think of as your blackest times."

When he was dropped to the ground, he stayed where he was. He knew her to be gone. The magic that had brought her to him was gone as well. But not the feeling that he'd been had. That he'd been tricked. He looked at Janell then.

"Nay, whatever goes into your head, I had nothing to do

with it. When I sat you there, the ground was clear of any garden. It was not until I saw what you were about that I realized that it was someone's magic." He knew that. She could no more lie to him than he could her. "You have been chosen, my lord. A great gift was given to you as well."

"I don't think of it as a gift, Janell. Did you not hear her say that a great many people would die? That I would have my heart broken many times while I waited for my mate to come to me?" She nodded. "Will you remain with me? Not leave my side while I have to go on living?"

"I must take to the ground for a time." He asked her why. "I need to rest. I have been, as were many other beings here, drained so that you might speak to the lady as you have. To hold her image for you is very taxing to my kind."

"What was she? And why did she pick me?" Janell said nothing. He wasn't sure if she was trying to keep from telling him the truth or if she didn't know. "How long will you leave me? When will you return?"

"I know not." He nodded and stood up. "You are lord now. You are aware of this, are you not? When your brother died, his lands and monies, they came to you."

"I've no wish of it." He didn't need it, either. What use could he have for lands and monies? "Take it for yourself."

"I shall protect it from others. I will rest on the land where he has died. The connection to the rest will be there for me." He didn't care and said as much to her. "You will someday, my lord. If for no other reason than when you take a mate."

"I won't. Not ever." He knew it for the lie that it was. "The lady, she said I was to have pain, pain that would bring me to my knees again. I won't have it, Janell. I can't stand pain like this again."

He wondered if his own mate would die before he could

convert her, and decided that he wasn't going to worry over something that was never going to happen. As he gathered what he could from the house, he made his way to talk with his parents. They would know that Malcomb was gone, as well as Mary, but he wanted to be with them. He would not talk of the lady that had come to him. Nor the magic that she'd given him. He would mourn the loss of his brother and then move on. Life was going to be on his terms, not that of a woman who had no name.

Richard

CHAPTER 1

"What have you found out? And if you give me an answer that I don't like, I'm going to put you into irons again, and this time I might forget all about you." Lucia waited for her sister — the fucking cunt was what she called her most of the time now — to say something. Anything. But she stood there, glaring at Lucia like she really didn't care if she did what she threatened.

As much as she hated to admit it, Lucia couldn't go very long without Ryiah around. There was something that she had, some sort of magic that sustained her. Not that she'd ever tell her sister that, but she needed her. The fucking cunt was going to pay someday. But for now, Lucia would let her think she was going to live as long as she did.

"You asked me to find him for you. I did that. There were no other orders given to me. So if you're finished, I'd like to go back to what I was —"

"Why the fuck would I have you find him if I didn't want you to tell me anything about him?" She slapped Ryiah across the mouth before she could think better of it. The pain on her own face nearly took her to her knees, but she'd not fall front in of Ryiah. There was no way she'd let her see her pain. "Get out of my sight. And don't come back until I call for you."

Hatred. There was so much of it coming off Ryiah that she thought she could bathe in it. When she finally turned and left, Lucia leaned back in her seat. Rubbing her cheek, the same side as the one she'd hit Ryiah on, burned in pain.

It was exhausting being around her sister, almost as much as it was fun. To see her hate so much, her loving and sweet sister, to be so angry all the time. It was almost worth pissing her off to see it. But she was no closer to knowing anything about Richard.

He was her mate. Lucia had been trying to end his family for centuries, and this one man had kept her from her goal. Every single time she had him in her sights, he'd manage somehow to get out of it with nothing more than a scorched shirt or a nick to his flesh. Never had one man vexed her as much as this single one had. She'd come to the conclusion that he was her mate. It only stood to reason that was why she couldn't harm him, and it was impossible for her to murder him.

"This 'causing no harm' rule is making me look bad." She looked at the man who was standing guard over her, and he didn't even look her way. She wondered if she were to send him after her betrothed whether he would have any better luck than she had in killing him. More than likely not. No matter what she threw at him, Richard would never fucking die.

She could kill his family. That had been no problem, and she'd done that, easily. Killing his first mate had been just as easy as ending the life of any human. The big bad Richard had been powerless to stop her from that. Murdering Angelica at her rest had been boring actually, but she had died. It had been Lucia's hope that, like his brother, Richard would not be able to stand the pain and would kill himself. Vampires could not live without their mates. But apparently he could.

There were other things that she'd tried as well, like catching him in his lair. The man didn't appear to have one. Nor did he need to rest during the daylight. And with his age, she'd not been able to guess when he'd need to feed next. He could go weeks before needing to find a human, and after a short time of watching him, she'd grow bored and miss it. The son of a bitch was not helping her out of this situation one bit, it seemed.

Getting up, she went to the window. Creatures were in the yard now, but most of them were dead or dying. Several weeks ago she'd been overrun with the things, all bent on coming into her compound. Now there were only a few, one or two a day. And even they seemed to be lackluster in their attempts to get at her. Even when she was in the yard, they were slow to move, as well as stupid. Whatever had made them had done a piss poor job of it.

Lucia knew that had she been in charge of such beings, she would have done things differently. First and foremost, they needed to be better dressed. They all looked the same, from their clothing to their facial expressions, which told her that they were monsters. Had they been in better clothing and even combed their hair, she was sure they could have ended the human race by now. Instead, they were only centering on one area, and even that didn't have nearly the amount of people that the rest of the world had in it. Maybe she'd go and find this leader and have a talk with him. Or perhaps not. If he were this stupid about creating things, she'd not want to speak to him. He'd give her a headache, and she had enough going on that was doing that to her at the moment.

Watching the yard, she noticed her sister there. What she was doing was a mystery to her. Not that Lucia cared, but if Ryiah was having fun or enjoying something, Lucia would put a stop to it. Lately, that had been harder to do. Her sister didn't seem to enjoy anything anymore.

"Serves her right in not dying when I wanted her to." Wiping at the window, Lucia pretended to remove Ryiah's head. "If only it were so easy, I would have done it long ago and be in full power with her magic."

Lucia looked around, and when she saw no one near her, she sat down and let her fear take her. She was very afraid of Ryiah. Terrified that someday she'd figure out that Lucia was the younger of them and not the oldest by the hour that really separated them. Her mother had had a plan, one that she was sure now she'd meant to profit from.

Her mother had told Lucia that if she wanted to get ahead, she must make her sister heel to her. For Ryiah's power was going to be great, and that once she came to her own, it would destroy all that Lucia wanted. Men would not adore her, nor would she be able to have the finest of things. And Lucia, even then, had wanted it all. The pretties that should be hers, her mother told her. Jewels and money, more than she'd be able to spend, would be hers for the taking, but only if she would take the place of her sister. Lucia hadn't understood that until Ryiah came into her power on their thirteenth birthday first. It had been something so grand and amazing that Lucia had been sorely disappointed when her turn came.

Hers had no bright lights before her eyes as her sister's had. No marking on her body had come to her, and no magic had come to her from the earth. Lucia was given more magic, yes, but not on the scale that her sister had. Lucia had been devastated. But her mother once again had stepped in and

24

helped her.

Shutting her away in the shed, her mother told Ryiah and anyone else who asked that Lucia was overwhelmed by the magic that had come to her, and she needed quiet to deal with it. When she'd been freed of her confines, people were disappointed that she looked no different. But Mother had said it was because Lucia was so beautiful, and that her magic wasn't something to take away from that.

It had broken Lucia's heart when she'd had to have her mother murdered by the Council. But she simply knew too much. Even when her mother told them what she'd done, screaming at Lucia to tell them, she'd turned her back on her only ally and decided that with her gone, there wasn't anyone to gainsay her on killing Ryiah. But that hadn't worked out either.

But by then she'd taught her sister that she was the stronger and by far more magical than Ryiah would ever be. Lies and deceit seemed to be easier for Lucia than telling the truth and being nice to Ryiah. Thankfully her sister had been beaten down so much over the previous years that Lucia hadn't had to do much to keep her there. Had she not done what she had, Lucia would be the one trailing after her sister, doing the worst jobs possible and hating her to the point where murder would be all that she thought about. Looking down at her sister now, Lucia saw her sit in the grass and look out among the trees, and she wondered what other things she could do that Lucia could not.

"She would never have treated me the way I do her. Her heart, at one time, was soft, and she too kind. Because she's a sap, I would have gotten some of what I wanted, but not all. Ryiah would have been kind with her magic. Sharing what she had with me. Keeping me in the manner that I wanted, and she'd never have harmed anyone." Lucia laughed. "She's very lucky that I was smart enough to know that to get ahead in this world, you have to cut a few heads off."

But what to do with Richard.

His family had been a pain in her ass since she was young. His brother first. Malcomb had shunned her twice when she'd gone to him about becoming his lover. Yes, she was younger than him, but she'd been beautiful. The magic that had been put on her to drive him crazy with lust had done nothing but anger him. He had a mate, he had told her, and she should go away.

It had been nothing for her to get someone to go and kill him. No one that worked for her would ever say no to her. But killing him had been...easy, she thought. Or at least his mate had been. Then Malcomb had done her a favor by killing himself. It was then that she found out about Richard, a brother that she never knew he had.

Trying the same magic on him had been useless. First of all, she had a difficult time finding the man. Then when she had, he'd been too busy to notice her. It had taken her nearly a century to find him after Malcomb had done her a favor and taken his own life. But by then Richard had come into his own.

His parents had met the sun, leaving Richard as the only heir to their vast estate soon after Malcomb was dead, and Lucia had wanted that as well. It could all be hers if she could only get him to acknowledge her as his mate. And now, it seemed, that was turning out to be a fact. Richard was her mate, damn it all to hell. Now she realized why she could not kill him as she wished. But the money would be hers, and that, for the moment, could keep her happy.

The plan had been simple. The paperwork and wills that had been made leaving her everything he had were perfect. All she needed to do was kill him, any way she could so long as he was ash and not around to gainsay her plans. Their names had been bound together by a faerie that was now long gone, and not there to say anything different. The faerie had signed the necessary things to say that they were mates and had bonded and mated. And once Richard was gone, she would bring the will and other paperwork before the Council, then claim his estate. It would go a long way to making sure that she had everything and anything she wanted. Even enough to hire someone to murder Ryiah once and for all.

The money that his family had and the magic that would come to her by taking him as a mate had made her reckless and foolish, she knew this now. Even when he'd taken another woman for his mate, someone so boring that Lucia had thought it a mistake, she plotted and planned. But when she'd gone into the bedchamber to drive the stake through both their hearts, it was to find a beauty lying next to Richard, and her jealousy had made her pause.

Richard had attacked her even as she shifted to another being to hide who she was from him. It had been all she could do to keep her head. As it was, she'd been hurt badly and had gone to ground soon after. But his mate was no more. She was sure that was going to be the end of the James family.

"My lady?" Lucia tore her eyes from the scene below her, not really seeing it any longer anyway. Her mind jerked from her memories as she stared at the woman in the doorway. She was confused for several seconds and had to have her repeat what she'd said to understand.

"So you've located him. When do you bring him to me?" The woman told her it wasn't possible. "What do you mean, not possible? I want him here. That alone should give you good reason to do as I say. Get him now."

27

"There is a spell around the dwelling where he is." Lucia looked at the ground below her where Ryiah was and then back at the woman. For the life of her, she had no idea what her name might be. "Nay, my lady. This is not the doing of Ryiah. This is a powerful magic that I have never encountered. Whatever it is, it is nothing that any of us have ever felt before. There is also a curse around it. One that says if there is ill will in your heart, you will not be able to cross the barrier." When she said no more, Lucia wondered if everyone was working against her in every little thing she had to do.

"So? If that's all it takes, then think of something else other than getting him for me. Think of...Christ, I don't know. Something. Anything that will get what I want." The woman shook her head and backed up when Lucia stood. "Do not tell me no. You know what that does to my temper. Go there, get him, and bring me Richard James today."

"I know the plan, my lady. It will know, this magic, that I'm there for a single purpose. I need only try to step my foot over the barrier and it will kick me back. Some have been killed for trying too many times." Lucia waited and crossed her arms over her chest when she did so. "You do not expect me to do that, do you, my lady? To get myself killed for you?"

"I expect you to do as you're told and to bring me Richard now. I don't want to hear excuses, and I certainly don't want to hear how you aren't giving it your best. Get him." As the woman turned and walked away, Lucia shouted to her, "You belong to me and you will do as you are told."

Sitting in her chair, Lucia tried to think how she was going to rid herself of Richard and his soon to be attachment to her. She couldn't kill him, much less harm him, so she had to think of a way to kill him once and for all. Ryiah would have to do it. That was the only way she could be assured of him being killed, and perhaps her sister being killed in the process. But how to make it come about? How to make her sister hate the man as much as she did and have her kill him?

"Perhaps I can pretend that he means something to me. That should get her motivated." No, that would work for her, but not Ryiah. She was simply too nice. "I shall send her for him. If she cannot get by the barrier, then she will die. One of them dead will suit me, and I can blame her death on Richard to the Council. It would be a win-win for me."

Calling for her sister to be brought to her, Lucia decided to practice her sorrow. It would not do for her to look gleeful at a time like that. She thought she had maybe a few days to look like she'd only just lost it all. Plenty enough time, she thought.

~~~

Rick wasn't sure he'd ever been this tired. But it was a good kind of tired. Something that of late, he'd not experienced too much of. Working in the gardens with the humans was providing his mind with a calmness that he'd never experienced before. And they weren't even planting anything until spring.

The lands had been tilled up just yesterday. Richard, like a great many of the people at the compound, had figured they were for graves. Not that anyone had died, but it seemed odd to him that the ground was being turned over — a term he'd had to ask what it meant — this late in the year. The next month it would be winter and they'd already seen their share of small white flakes coming down, so a garden had never entered his mind as to what they were preparing for.

"We've been able to find seeds to plant when the time is right. But the land, we're not sure that it can hold it in her to give us anything after we plant the seeds. They might be too old or not anything that grows in this area." The people, coming together at Remy's request, had been asked what they needed to do to make improvements. Betterment, he'd called it, of the area and the people living there. "We get plenty of canned goods from the stores now, but there are little to no fresh things. We wanted to grow a few things and perhaps sell them to the stores for those who can't have a garden."

Remy had approved the garden, which everyone figured he would, but he'd gone a little further in his quest and had people use some of the abandoned equipment to till up not just the plot of land that Rick was working, but also the land of anyone that wanted their own personal garden at their new homes. Everyone had been thrilled with the idea. So today, his day off, Rick had gone out to see how it was going, and had been helping before he knew it.

"Do you suppose that when spring comes, the time to plant the seeds, that anyone will still have an interest in this project?" He looked over at Nate, who had been coming out more and more of late. "I, for one, would love to taste a tomato that I pick fresh. Eat it out here in the sunshine while I sprinkle each bite with a bit of salt."

"A childhood memory?" Nate nodded and moved carefully around the people there with him. "You do know that no one is as afraid of you as you are of them. They just don't care that you're huge so long as you talk calmly and don't hit them."

"Very funny. And I'm still weak. Well, weak is the wrong word, I suppose. I'm as strong as an ox. But I still have moments when my body betrays me somehow, and I find myself flat on my ass and not knowing just how I got there. I think it's still a growing phase or something. Like when I was a child between being a kid and puberty." Rick nodded and leaned on the hoe that he'd been using. "I have leveled out in my weight, I think. I'm consuming about six thousand calories a day now, and that's been consistent for the last week. And I've been doing as you asked about the tat on my back too. There are differences. Every day I can see something more."

"Good to know. And Remy said that you're coming along with your sword play as well. Said that he can't knock you to the ground as easily." Nate only nodded and looked around. "Do you have a mind to grow something here?"

"No. I just wanted to get out a little." But there was something on his mind. Nate and he weren't friends, not by a long shot. But Nate had learned, the hard way, he supposed, that Rick would be honest with him, even if it hurt him. "There is a woman coming. Today or tomorrow, I think. I was playing with the computers when I saw her there. She's hurt."

"Lucia?" He had told Nate about her, one night when he was so angry it had taken him hours to calm his blood. Nate shook his head, then nodded. "I see. Well, that's very clear and helpful. Do you suppose you could narrow it down a little? Perhaps give me a hint what you mean?"

"Lucia, what does she look like? Do you think her beautiful?" He told him he'd never seen the woman, but had heard that she was pretty. Maybe even beautiful. "This woman that comes here soon, she's more than beautiful. She has a way about her, too, that makes me think that she's pure of heart. And of body, if you know what I mean."

"I do. She's a virgin. Do you think that she's coming here to cause us harm?" Nate said nothing and Rick let him remain quiet as he dug in the dark rich earth. He could smell it, this fertile land, and wanted to bury his body in it and remain there for a long while. Rick thought it would be a wonderful thing to have it wrapped around him.

"I think she's trouble. Not trouble, but she will cause it. I have no idea why." Rick said nothing as he turned another spade of the dark rich dirt over. "But there is something very sad about this person."

"Did you talk to one of the others? The ones that can read the earth?" Nate said that he hadn't, but might. "It would be good to know what we're about to encounter. Perhaps she might be your mate. If she's as beautiful as you say, maybe you'll be all right."

"No. I can't have a mate. I would crush a woman should I try to make love to her."

Rick said nothing. He knew that having a mate, no matter her size, there would always be ways of making love. Rick continued on his job, thinking of the woman who may or may not be coming here to claim him. Lucia was going to be in for a huge surprise if she thought to try and make him her mate. He'd surely murder her. Gladly.

"I talked to the Council as you had suggested. About Lucia coming here because she found out what I'd done to her." Nate asked him what they had said to him. "They said that after so many years the records are made public, but that no one, not anyone, has come to see who had turned Lucia in for murder and her use of magic. They said that in order for her to see them, for anyone to see them, they'd have to get permission first, then they'd have to be watched by one of them as they went over them."

"So she might not know it was you. Or she's not figured out that she could look. I did a little looking myself. Not that anyone would ever know it, but I did look. Lucia had been found guilty, as you'd been told, but only on a lesser charge. That of living with a nest of vampires. I didn't know that was a crime. Anyway, she had all these letters of good conduct, as well as a few things that showed her being a good and respectable faerie. I thought that she fabricated them, but I guess they thought of that too. Apparently they were real and the people had only good things to say about her." Rick nodded. Janell had found that out for him as well. "Why can't a faerie live with a bunch of your kind?"

"Faerie blood is like a powerful drug to us, and highly addictive. It hypes us up in a way like...well, like you are right now, at least the strong part. Powerful yes, but stupid too. But it only lasts for a short time, and the more we take of it, the more we need until we change with it. And not in a good sort of way. Nests have been known to murder thousands of humans just for the pure pleasure of seeing them bleed out after getting the mind drugging blood from one faerie. I don't know how she managed to survive if she was living with them." He thought of the one taste of faerie that he'd ever had. "Our vision is better, even better than we have now. Our strength is about four times that of an old vampire, and we can do things, magic that the faerie had when bitten, for a short time as well. It's very dangerous. I'm betting she was getting something from them in return for whatever they wanted of her. Or that she murdered them and failed to mention that in the event that she might get into more trouble. From what I've heard of her, Lucia watches out very carefully for herself."

"Why do you think she's your mate, Rick?" He continued to hoe the dirt, trying to think of an answer to any of the one million questions he'd asked himself when Nate continued. "She's not at all like you. Not from what I've heard from people. According to the reports written about her, even before you reported her, she was evil. Killing for no apparent reason. Robbery as well as magical fraud. That, too, I had to look up. She killed lesser beings for their magic when there was nothing to gain from it. She has this group, a gang—I'm not sure what you call a group like she has other than a gang—that does whatever she says with no questions asked. They've been linked to several murders; even before this started, they were killing humans daily. Why would a faerie need to murder a human? I thought they were like one with the earth or something."

"They don't. Not usually. But Lucia was...I want to say she wasn't like her family, but that's not true. Her father had been a war faerie back in the day. I think Lucia was too for a while, but she became less of one that would show up on a field to turn the tide and more a faerie that would rob the dead and take from the living. I have since found out that many years ago, long before wars were fought with guns but with swords, she was stripped of her title and had been reduced to a simple faerie. It was the ruination of her family too, this demotion of sorts." He'd known her father and thought him a good man. It was his mate that Rick had hated, almost as much as he did her child. "Luke, her father, had millions of faeries at his command. It was said that at one time if he and his men were to show up at a battle, both sides would lay down their weapons for fear that they'd be fighting a losing war against him."

"Okay, so he spawned this child that became a monster. What of the other daughter?" Rick paused in his memories and looked at Nate. "There was another child, a daughter born the same day. Her name eludes me at the moment, but there were twins born of Luke and Celia. She is only mentioned in the records that I had Kate and Chris look into for me as the firstborn, but nothing else can be found about her. So while we know that she's alive, there is no record of her as being a part of the earth."

"I don't understand." Nate told him what he knew. "So this child, twin of Lucia, is sort of a ghost? No one knows anything about her, nor where she might be? You know that the only way for her not to be a part of the earth is for her to have spent her time in stone without sun. Or someone has some powerful magic around her."

"I know that now, but I'm telling you that there is nothing about her in the earth. And not only that, but according to Chris, not only is Lucia the second born, but she's weaker than she's let anyone know about. Her magic is there, but not nearly as powerful as she's let anyone believe. Oh, and there is something else. When I had Chris look into the deaths that she is responsible for—and I had to ask him exactly what I wanted—she killed your sister-in-law as well as your mate. Your brother's death was a direct result of his mate dying, so I guess you could say that she had something to do with that as well."

Rick never felt the hoe drop from his hand. Didn't know what it meant to have the dirt he'd been working in come up so quickly to his face. As his mind shut down, all he could think about was that Lucia had killed his family and that she was going to pay. Then his mind went blank.

Richard

CHAPTER 2

Ryiah moved along the road toward the encampment without a thought as to what she was supposed to do when she got there. It was easier for her, at least when she was doing the bidding of her sister, to not think. It was too painful to believe that her sister thought so very little of her that she'd think that Ryiah was disposable like this. Instead she watched the woman that had been following her for the last hour move from house to house. Then when there wasn't one, from tree to tree.

If she was trying to hide from her, she was doing a very poor job of it. Tiring of the cat and mouse game, Ryiah stopped walking and turned to where she was hiding this time. As she came out from behind the large tree, Ryiah figured out what she was.

"I'm sorry." The woman asked her for what. "I thought.... Well, it matters little what I think. But you can tell Lucia that I'm doing as she commanded, and that I do not need a spy to report back to her."

"I'm no spy for Lucia. I wish her dead, if you want to

know the truth of the matter. She and I are not friends either, so I would not do her bidding if she were to ask me to." There was a lot of that going around, but Ryiah didn't speak. This too could be a trap to be reported back to her sister. "Do you know this...I suppose I should call her a woman, for lack of a better description. But do you know her well?"

"I do." The woman looked around but said nothing more. "Why are you spying on me if not to tell her if I do what she makes me?"

"I work for a person that wishes to know what she's about. If she has ordered you to do something, then I should like to know what it is. I know that I am not to speak to you like this, but I should really like to have some news to tell him." Ryiah asked her why she'd not be able to speak to her. "You are a faerie of great magic, a war faerie if I have it right. I am only a lesser faerie that serves a vampire."

"I'm not Lucia." The woman smiled and said that she knew that. "My name is Ryiah, not Lucia. I mean, I know you said you know that, but I'm not a war faerie. That would be her."

"Perhaps she is, but you are one as well." Before she could shake her head and tell her she was wrong again, the woman continued. "My name is Janell. I had, at one time, adopted a last name, but I have since forgotten it. Not that it matters, I guess, but there you have it. You are a war faerie. As surely as I am standing here, I can tell. And you have been wounded by a lesser faerie as recently as today, and you are hoping that you die when you make it to the compound. I'm sorry, my lady, but I can only tell you the truth because of what you are."

"No. I don't know...is this a trick? Did Lucia send you here to trick me? To get me to say something that she can punish me for? I assure you that her beatings don't bother me as much as she thinks they do. It has become so tedious that I just take them and go on about my business. I mean, maybe if she were to change it up some. But I guess because she believes it works, why mess with it. I'm sorry. That's more information than you want, I guess." Janell assured her that she wasn't there to spy on her. "Then someone has sent you. What are you about? Why are you telling me these falsehoods?"

"I cannot lie to you, mistress. You know that as well as I do." Ryiah looked around. There had to be a trap somewhere. Someone was trying to make her go back to the cell, bound there for all eternity. It wouldn't be so bad, but Lucia had also taken the soil and the sunlight from her. "You're her sister, aren't you? The older sister to the monster of the house?"

Ryiah backed away but didn't get far before she felt arms tighten around her. They were strong in muscle, but she could feel the powerful magic too. Standing as still as she could, she begged the man behind her not to harm her any more.

"But if you must, then I would prefer that you take my head off my shoulders. I assure you that I shan't fight you. In fact, I could have a sword brought to you that is sharp and — "

"I can smell your blood, fresh and strong. How badly are you hurt?" She told him it wasn't that bad. "Yet you beg me not to harm you more. Or if I wish, to kill you, you will have a sword brought to me. Which is it? Do you feel brave enough to take me on, or are you in too much pain for me to touch?"

She looked around and up. The man was tall, taller than any that she'd ever encountered before. But the humor in his voice, the way he smiled at her, had her thinking he might be addled in his head as well. When he laughed, she felt the heat of her embarrassment on her face and told him she was sorry. But if she had to tell him why she was there, perhaps she could ask also for a place to stay. If only for a little while.

"I have been sent to find a man. One that my sister, as you know now, is looking for." He nodded but didn't let her go. "You know him, I think. And I you. Rembrandt the Warrior, are you not?"

"I've been called many a name, my good woman. Too many for me to track should I even have a desire to." She'd heard that as well. This was a good man. "This man you seek. It is perchance, Rick?"

"Nay, his name is Richard. Richard James, the second lord of the Highland castles of Ireland." Rembrandt looked at Janell, then back down at her. Then her embarrassment doubled when she realized what he'd asked her. "I only just remembered that Rick could be short for Richard. Am I correct in assuming this is the same man?"

"You might be. But if he has a title, no one has mentioned it before now. I think perhaps we have been remiss in getting information about him. You say your sister has sent you to come for him. What does she want with one of my friends?" Ryiah felt her heart twist up at the way the man seemed very protective of the man she was to get at all costs. It was in his heart that Richard...Rick...was a man that he felt worth dying for. If only she had such a friend. "You should know that with my touch, I can read your mind easily, Ryiah. And I am sorry for your loss."

"You can only see what I let you see. And knowing my name will get you nothing." When she pulled from him, he allowed her to. Ryiah wasn't stupid enough to think that she'd forced his hand. "My sister is Lucia. Lucia Alvarez. It is her plan to have me bring him to her. Then she will bind us together as one would mates and hope that we kill one another. There would be no blood bond for us to hold back, and then she would be rid of us both, or so that is her plan. She hates me as much as she does him."

"Do you know the reason for such a hatred?" She asked him if he meant her or Rick. "Both. I should like to know why a sister would wish her own dead. And a man, from all accounts, that she has never met."

"Her wish to see me dead is because she thinks me to be hers to rule. And since I have become less inclined to listen to her, much less heed her commands, she tires of me and I of her. Death, I suppose, is the only way for the bonds of blood to be cut." Rembrandt said nothing but watched her. "I have...I no longer wish to serve her. I have a desire, almost as much as she does for me, to become one with the earth. To die and let the soil hold me within her arms forever. I believe it would be much warmer than her, and more comforting as well. But I also have no desire to let her think she has won."

"So you don't let yourself die, even though I'm sure she has tried many times, out of spite?" Ryiah felt herself responding to his humor and smiled at him. "I like you, Ryiah. I truly do. But Rick is on call today and out cleaning up some of the malefactors that have gotten themselves into some trouble."

"Malefactors?" He explained what they were. "The creatures have been lower in numbers. I had wondered why. You and your army, they have taken out a great many of them."

"We've tried. And yes, there are a great many less of them than when we began. Does their touch bother you?" She told him that she'd never encountered one until today, that she'd been in a cell until recently. "By your sister's hand, no doubt. And what does she think you did to be deserving of such horrid conditions?"

"Live." He nodded as if he understood. There were

41

times when she didn't understand at all, but was glad for his comments to her. "Rick is to be brought to her by me. But should you shackle me in iron and take me to your dungeon, I cannot do anything about it. I will be...I think I should be safe for the first time since I was born."

She couldn't lie to him. Not that she'd even try, but she found that she wanted to be imprisoned by this man. She knew that while she would be in a cell again, he would not be so cruel to her that he'd take away the very things that made her live. Both the sun and the soil would not just heal her, but she could feed from them as well if necessary.

"I think we can do better than that. While you have a task in your heart, ill-will toward one of my men, I think you will have no problem crossing the barrier that keeps most evilness out. Come, let us go back to the compound and see about this lordship that you've been searching for." She followed him to a great vehicle. She'd seen them around but had never ridden in one. When she stood by the opening, Ryiah felt the world close around her.

"I should like to fly there, if you don't mind. The thought of being closed up in that thing makes me afraid." He closed the door and let his own wings go. "I have my own, but should you feel better about taking me, I shall not fight you."

"Will you come with me then?" She nodded and told him she was his prisoner. "You're not, but all right. If that is the way we have to work this, for now you can be my prisoner. Come, Ryiah, I should like to see your wings."

When she let them go, he stood there staring at her. After a time, he asked her to turn and she did. When she faced him again, he was staring at Janell and she felt fear again. Perhaps he wanted the other woman to kill her. Ryiah dropped to her knees and stretched out her neck. This was dying with as much grace as she could get.

~~~

Rick could see Remy and Janell. He had a moment of anger that Remy would be talking to his friend, but he saw the other woman with them. Rick had no idea why he'd thought for just a moment that Remy was going behind his back and gaining information, but it was gone almost as soon as it formed. He moved slowly to them just as the woman dropped to her knee and looked as if she were awaiting her head to be removed. When he was standing between Janell and Remy, he asked what was going on.

"This woman here has been sent to fetch Richard James, the second lord of the Highland castles of Ireland. I don't suppose you might know who that is, do you?" He looked at Janell and started to ask her why she'd tell them that when Remy laughed as he continued. "Janell had nothing to do with this. This woman here has told us. She is the sister to Lucia."

Without thought as to how he might harm her, Rick jerked up the young woman and held her above the ground by her throat. She neither struggled nor tried to pull his hand away, but stared at him as if begging him to kill her. Remy cleared his throat, but didn't tell him to let her down.

"She is under the rule of Lucia, and has already volunteered to become a resident of our dungeons. I'm sure that the building can put one in should we desire it, but I've no idea why she'd be thinking of such a thing." Remy moved to stand in front of him, the girl between them. "Should you wish to snap her neck, I think it would do you no good. But if it would, then we'd be no closer to finding answers about Lucia than we were before. Mayhap if you put her down for a moment or two, she could give us some."

"Lucia killed my mate. And my brother's mate before his

grief made him end his own life. I should like to show her what it feels like to lose someone very dear to her heart." Remy told him that Lucia would not care about this one. He also doubted very much that many would care about the death of the one he held. "What do you mean, not care? This is her sister, her blood. Family is all that you can have in your life. Of course she would care if I killed her."

"Let her down, Rick, and let her tell you in her own words. I'm sure that they're different than the things going on in your own head right now." Rick glanced at Nate, who had been working with him, when he spoke again. "She might be able to clear up some of the things that I was telling you about yesterday. Besides, I can smell fresh blood. She's hurt enough without you trying to take her head off with your bare hands."

He dropped her. And if he expected her to get up and try to harm him, he was disappointed. All she did was curl into a tight ball and lay there. It was then that he saw the blood on her back. Turning her to her belly, he nearly fell back when he saw the damage done to her.

"She does not order me to be whipped. There is a law that states that she can do me no harm without cause. But she has a man that roams her home that has been told that if he sees me, he is to take me to the wall and beat me. Not her direct words. She cannot harm me. But she had told this man that everyone he sees should be whipped. He has noticed that he gets a bigger bonus when I am hurt. So now I am all that he finds." Rick asked her how long this had been going on. "Forever, I think. If you would be so kind as to take me to the cell now, I will give you no trouble."

Rick bent to pick her up, but her screams had him nearly dropping her again. When she was calm, her body limp in his arms, he knew that she had fainted and looked at Remy for guidance. He had no idea what to do now.

"She said that she can't ride in the car. I think she's been confined before, and the thought of it has her avoiding it at all costs. If you hand her to me, I shall — "

Rick felt his inner beast roar up. "Don't touch her." Janell stepped between him and faced Remy before turning to him. As he held the woman to him, he could see that Janell understood whatever was going on better than he did. Still he told her what he felt. "She cannot be touched by him. I can't allow it."

"She is the one?" He nodded, not sure what she would think of this when she laughed. "We only knew that she was coming. And that she was blood of Lucia. Had I any idea that she had a sister, I might have looked closer. This one, she will complete you."

"I've no desire to be completed. I have had my chance at love, and her sister destroyed it all for me." Janell only looked to the sky when it darkened over them. As soon as Skylar touched the earth, Rick pulled the woman's body closer to him. "I cannot allow you to harm her."

"Well, that's good. I don't know why you'd jump to that conclusion, but I'm only here to take her to the compound. I understand that she's your mate." Rick said nothing but felt his anger at them all double. "Take it down a notch there, buck-o. I'd hate to have to hurt you over this. I'm not going to hurt her, nor am I going to stand here while you try and get your head out of your ass and figure that this is a done deal. Just hand her over and I'll make sure that she's taken care of."

"She's not my mate. Her sister killed my family." Before he could think of her intent, Skylar took the woman from him and was gone. Rick looked at Remy. "What am I to do with a mate that, every time I think of her sister and what she's done to me, I want to kill her?"

"Think of something else. Until you know what is going on, you cannot place the blame at a door that's not been opened for you. She may be a pawn. And so that you are aware, I believe her to be just that, a pawn to get you killed." Rick pointed out that they were related. "Aye, they are. As was our Vicki to her brother."

As he was left standing there with Nate, he wondered why it was that Remy could be so fucking calm about this. The woman was a war faerie, someone that could have them all killed at a moment's notice.

Something flew by his face, and just as he was going to swat at it, his hand was stayed by magic.

"Hello." He nodded at the...the bug? "No, not quite. I'm a faerie. You've seen some of my kind around. Only I think you thought us all bugs. We're not bugs. Faerie. Say it with me. Fae—rie."

"I know what you are." She only tisked at him. "Would you let me go, please? I don't care to be held when I've done nothing to warrant it."

"Yes. But you must promise to look before you swat. It might be my grandmother, and she will not be pleasant about being hit away. While old, she's as mean as a brownie when they've been told there is an early frost. Not a pretty sight, let me tell you." He made the promise and felt his arm freed. "Now. I've been sent by the queen to ask you if you have any idea what you've gotten into here. Or for that matter, what's to come."

"Into? I'm not sure what.... What queen are you talking about? England?" She laughed at him and flittered around until she was on his hand. Holding her up to see her, he was amazed at how lovely she was. "What are you?"

"Fae—rie." Rick wasn't in the mood for this shit and dropped his hand and turned his back on her. "I'm sorry, my lord, but I was only trying to make you smile. You have a lovely smile, and perhaps my lady will like you better should you smile once in a while. You do that so seldom that I did wonder if you were hiding something. Fangs, yes, I know that, but I thought perhaps you had bad breath and that you were keeping it behind your teeth. You could get ill from that, I think. But then—"

"Enough!" He heard birds fly away, screaming at him for the disturbance. But the little bug just smiled at him as she balanced herself in front of his face. "I'm going to ask you questions and you'll answer them without going all over the city and back before you get to it. All right?"

"Yes. I would like to say that I only upset you to get your attention. You can focus more on me now that you're over your snit." She looked around. "Do you suppose we could go somewhere that I can land? Flying like this is exhausting. And I shan't land on you again, because you can be most cruel when you're upset."

He found himself in his room with her. Rick thought of all the things that had been going on lately. The things with Benton. The horde of malefactors and figuring them out. There was magic everywhere now. But sitting in his room with a faerie flying around looking at his books and pictures was the freakiest of it all.

"My name is Hunter. I hunt, so that's what I was called. My sister is Rose because she takes care of the roses. There are thousands of us, and we all have specific jobs." He leaned back in the chair to try and wrap his mind around the things that had happened in the last hour. "You should know that Ryiah had nothing to do with your family. She was in a prison cell."

"Who is Ryiah?" He thought he knew, but she confirmed it. "So Ryiah is the sister to Lucia, who I thought was my mate. If you don't mind me saying so, this is really fucked up."

"Aye, it is. And Lucia believes you to be her mate as well. It is what we all wanted her to believe. So that she'd send Ryiah here to get you someday. The rest of us have failed to bring you to her, you see. It was on purpose, but she did as we thought and now she's safe. If you don't toss her away again." He asked her why as she sat down on the edge of his bed in front of him. "So that she would be happy and with you. It's a good thing that we hurried things along a little more. Lucia wishes her sister dead, and if she had put her in the cell again, Ryiah would have taken her own life and there would have been little we could have done about it. She would have just let her body shut down until she was no longer."

"She said that she didn't care for closed in places. This cell she was in, how small was it?" An image appeared in front of him and he could see Ryiah there, curled into a tight ball in the corner. The cell, dark and damp, was smaller than his bed, which was only a full. There were no windows, no lights at all. The only place where there might have been light was blocked off. He wondered how she would even get anything to eat. "For what reason would she do this to her own flesh and blood?"

"She cannot kill her. Nor can she directly harm her. And in answer to your thoughts, she did not feed her at all. I took her what I could, but it was barely enough to keep her going. She might have died if not for me. There is a man, one that beats her regularly, but he is paid to beat all the people within the house and gets a bonus should he hurt Ryiah." Hunter moved around his room again. "You have many books here.

48

Do you read them all?"

"I do. This mate thing, so you arranged it so that she'd be my mate? I mean, she's not really that, just the appearance of it, so that she could escape her sister?" She stopped flying and came back to sit on his knee. "It's all right if you did. I've buried my mate. I have no need to do so for another. And I understand that you wanted her to be safe. So do I, now that she's here."

"She is your true mate, my lord. Lucia believes what she does because all her attempts to kill you have been thwarted. It is because you have been protected." He asked her by who. "The queen. She marked you a very long time ago and now you belong to her. I think you do remember that, do you not?"

"The woman that came to where my sister-in-law was murdered. By Lucia." She nodded. "And you're saying that her sister had nothing to do with this? She had no part in any of my family being killed?"

"Nay. As I have said, she was held as a prisoner." He asked her what she'd done. "Refused to kill your family."

CHAPTER 3

Ryiah lay as still as she could, but still it was hard for her mind not to think. The man, the one that had nearly taken off her head, was sitting in the chair near the bed she was on, but he only stared. She was sure that he'd long since forgotten she was there.

He was handsome. His face reminded her of the pictures she'd seen of the great art exhibits around the world, hand carvings of nude men that had fought many wars and had come away hardened, not just of body but of mind as well. Ryiah knew he was a vampire and that he was old, more than a thousand years, but he wasn't jaded like the others that she knew. Hard, but not jaded. She could also see the markings on his neck, and wondered where else the man had been touched by the queen.

"My back as well." Ryiah nodded and watched his face as he sat there. "She told me that I would not be able to die. That she had plans for me. Something about someone coming to me that would be strong, and that I would love her. That it would last all through eternity."

"My sister." He shook his head. "She is most powerful. And she is your mate. I don't know why she'd think this, as she has never met you, but Lucia seldom is wrong. And if she is, then she kills whatever dares not to be right for her."

"She sounds like a wonderful being, this sister of yours." Ryiah said nothing. Sometimes she got sarcasm. She was sure that was what he was using, but she wasn't positive enough to agree or disagree with him. "I was being sarcastic."

"You can read my mind." He nodded and leaned his head back on the chair. Now she could see more of his mark. "The queen, she made it so that you could not be beheaded, and that anyone who would try to bite you without permission will suffer greatly for it. If you turn and remove your shirt, I can tell you the rest."

"You're my mate." She shook her head and realized that he could not see her, and told him it was Lucia. "No. It's you. I'm not sure why they did it, but the little faeries, one in particular named Hunter, told me that it was you all along, and that they wanted Lucia to believe that she was mine so she'd send you here. I think we've been set up."

"Lucia tried to kill you, she told me, and that you kept coming out of it unscathed." He looked at her then. "You have a beautiful face. I'm sure you know that, but you are very handsome."

"Are you always this forthright?" Ryiah wasn't sure what he meant by that, but did sit up on the bed. "There is juice there for you. Ann made it fresh from fruit and not a can. I'm sure you can tell the difference."

"I can." She picked up the glass and drained it. When she sat it down on the little table, she noticed that there were two more glasses of it, as well as a pitcher with condensation on it. "I have not had fresh fruit juice in a very long time. I shall have to thank her for this."

She drank down two more glasses, and then realized that the others were all full again. Instead of asking him about it, she decided that it must be the house proper. It was covered in magic, some of it as old as she was. Looking at him again as she sipped her fifth glass, she wondered why he seemed so out of sorts and asked him about it.

"Lucia killed my brother's wife, and then he met the sun rather than to live without her. I was there when someone came to the house, I discovered later, and set fire to the curtains in their room. Then they rammed a stake into her heart and tried to kill Malcomb. My own mate, Angelica, was murdered as well. Years later, however. I only just found out that your sister was responsible for all their deaths, and that she has plans to end my life as well. Do you know why?" She did and nodded. "I'm not sure I want to know all the reasons right now, but could you just give me the highlights?"

"Money. The power that comes with your age. There are a great many that would work for Lucia should she have the funds to pay them. Also, she hopes that with no bond between the two of us, she can order me to your bed and you will kill me. Or I will kill you. Either way, the other would be taken to the Gathering and found guilty of murder." She watched his face as she continued. "At one time she was a war faerie, like our father, but something happened and she was discharged of her duties. It must have been bad because usually a war faerie lives on forever in their position." He got up to pace and she thought him taking his anger out on his steps. "When she was sent home in disgrace, there was a man there. His surname was James. I believe now that he might be related to you. You are Richard James, are you not? However, this man, he is the one that stripped her of her armor and then disbursed her army. By then there were too few to call an army…less than five thousand strong. Some had left her service; others had been killed because she was reckless and cruel to them. Most left on the fields when she would kill both combatants instead of taking a side. In my father's day, he had tens of thousands to command. Are you the same family as this man?"

"Yes, my father. And I'm Rick to most people who know me. My dad, he was a great leader as well, and helped with the Faerie Council on occasion. I don't know the details of that particular event, but I'm sure that he would have been the one to do it. Most of the Council were afraid of their own shadows. Are they still?" She told him she'd never been before them, except when her sister called her there to witness for her. "Lucia has. Several times. I turned her in for her part in the killing of a thousand people who were trying to make a living in a small town. She murdered them all for no other reason than she could, I guess."

"That would be her." Ryiah got up when he sat. Going to the window, she let out a long breath. It was hard to be so closed up like this, and being near an opening helped her a great deal, even if it was covered in glass. "I'm not sure why you believe me to be your mate. I'm sure that you're mistaken. I know that you associate smell with this, but perhaps you can smell my sister on me and that has you confused."

"Come here." She looked at him and wondered why she thought him beautiful. He was an Adonis. A man like no other. When she stood up, he unbuttoned his shirt and when he took it off, he tossed it to the bed. Ryiah felt her mouth go dry and her tongue thicken. "Come here so that I can smell only you. I would like to get this cleared up as well."

"I'm afraid of you. Not that you'd harm me, but that you are…what should happen to me should you be wrong?" He told her he wasn't. "But if you are, will you please kill me?"

"No. Come here, Ryiah." She found herself moving toward him even as she had it in her head to stay put. As soon as she was within inches of him, he touched his fingers to her cheek and she felt it to her feet. "I don't know how this is to work, you being a faerie and me a vampire. We're to be sworn enemies, you and I."

His touch was doing things to her she'd never experienced before. And as much as she wanted to back away from him, she wanted to be closer as well. When he cupped her bottom and pulled her to him, her hands moved up his bare chest and over his hard nipples. Leaning down, Ryiah took one of the pert morsels into her mouth before she could think about what she was doing.

He pulled her closer, his hard male part rocking into her softness, and she moaned. Letting go of her treat, she looked up at him and could see the blood of his eyes, the desire, too, that was strong enough that she thought she could touch it. When he lowered his head to hers, Ryiah had a moment of panic, but he stilled just before touching his mouth to hers.

"Tell me no and I'll stop this now. But so you are aware, you're my mate as much as I am yours." His breath was warm, sweet smelling, and full of promise. "You keep thinking things like that and I will show you the promise that I have in my mind for you."

"Will you take me?" His breath came out in a soft rush. "I think I should like to feel you between my legs. Feel you filling me as a man should a woman. To have you suckle at my breast. Feed from me. I know not where these thoughts come from, but I should very much like to have you do them to me."

His kiss was soft, just a touching of the lips to hers. But

when he lifted his head and looked down at her, she grew hungry. For him. Pulling him back to her mouth, his body nearly consuming her in his heat, she mimicked his kiss and felt his strong hunger like her own. The next time their mouths met, Ryiah knew that he'd been right. She was his.

Her back touched the bed, and he was there for her. Even as her clothing was torn from her, she touched him wherever she could reach…his back, his arms, even his belly. She knew that his left ear was pierced. He bore a scar on his back that was old. A fresh one, smaller but no less ragged on his left side, had her wanting to explore it, ask him what had occurred. Then he took her breast into his mouth and bit down on her.

Her body detonated, came apart as he rode her softness through his pants. Even as he suckled hard enough to bring her again, she knew there was more. And Ryiah wanted it all. When he put her hand over his hardness, she felt him thicken. She thought of him naked and he suddenly was, and she felt his cock as he filled her hand and spilled over it. He was large and thick. Every part of her wanted not to just see him but to taste him, feel him inside of her.

"I need you." She nodded, telling him that she did him as well. "You've never had sex before? No man has ever touched you? I can smell your virginity, but I want to know how experienced you are about sex. Has any man touched you sexually?"

"Nay, I know not a lot of men that would dare to breach my rooms." She looked down his body at the part of him that leaked over her hand. "I should like to taste you here. To have you fill my mouth with your juices."

He rocked harder into her hand. Her own body was heating; her softness was wet and needy. Her juices were running down to her bottom and making her squirm a little by the heat of it. When he pulled back she sat up, thinking that he might be leaving her. But instead, he dropped to his knees in front of her and put her legs on either side of his head.

"I'm going to eat you." That sounded wonderful, and she watched him as he lowered his head to her. "I'm going to drink from you here, from your pussy. Then I'm going to come inside of you when I fuck you. When I do, Ryiah, I'm going to bite you as well."

"May I bite you?" He nodded, his fingers moving over her pussy, and she moaned. "Touch me, Rick, please. I feel so close to something that I want you to give me."

He slid inside of her, his fingers an invasion that made her see stars and need more. When he told her to lie back, she did so and brushed her hands over her full breasts. It felt so good to touch herself that she cupped them in her palms and squeezed her nipples. But when he took her into his mouth, her womanhood suckled hard and his fingers dancing, she came again, this time screaming out her release, as there seemed to be no room within her body for such enjoyment.

~~~

Rick knew that he should stop, that it was too much for her the first time. But she was coming so prettily for him, filling him in ways that no one ever had before. As she came a third, then a fourth time, he slid another finger into her to stretch her for him. The thought of hurting her, even in this, was painful to his heart.

When her fingers curled into his hair and lifted him from her, he watched her face. It was lovely. Beautiful in her sexual bliss. He wanted to paint her this way. Not on canvas. No canvas would ever be enough to capture her in such a beautiful way. He would paint her, rub a brush of silk over her and watch her enjoy it.

"Please. I need you." He stood, his cock so painfully full that he held himself. Fisting his cock so that he might come on her rather than take her this way, Rick moved onto the bed again and between her thighs. "You ache to fill me, do you not?"

"I do. I should like nothing better than to slam my cock deep into your pussy and never leave." He rubbed the tip of his cock over her clit and watched her juices slide over him. "The next time I have you, I'm going to feed from your pussy while you come down my throat. I wanted only for you to have pleasure this time, but the next, it will be for me."

"Please, Rick. I need more from you." He slid the tip of his cock, just the crown, into her. Rick watched her face, the excitement and the need taking her. She lifted her feet to wrap her legs around his hips, and he smiled when she pulled him forward, but he was still careful of his cock coming into her. "Fill me. Now."

The command had him slamming forward. He wanted to believe that she'd made him, used compulsion on him to do it, but he knew that his body was just as needy as hers. When she screamed, this time in obvious pain, he held her hips as he felt her body stretching for his cock. To move now would cause her more pain, and he just couldn't do that to her.

"Don't move." He told her he wouldn't, not until she was ready for him to. "I don't know that I will be. You're much bigger than I thought. And you fill me up to my throat, too."

"Thank you, but I know you can take me." He rolled his hips gently, trying to move to a better position to pull from her. But she cried out, her body bowing up off the bed as she came quick and hard. "You come so wonderfully. To watch your body when you release is a pleasure I could watch forever."

"You should do that again. When you move inside of me

like you did, I swear I can feel it all the way to my toes." Rick moved, slowly this time, to make sure that she felt every inch of him. "Yes. Again, please. That was wonderful."

He fucked her slowly, feeling each of the tight muscles in her sheath as she held him; the way her body hugged him tightly, seemingly sucking him deeper into her. Rick loved to watch her hands fill with her breasts, the way her nipples darkened just before she came. And when she was close, so close that a single movement from him could take her over the edge, her breaths became fast pants, and he wanted to sample every part of her.

"I need you to kiss me." He leaned down, and instead of taking her mouth, he suckled at the tip of her breast, nibbling none too gently on her nipple before biting hard enough to draw blood. He knew that she was aware that he was feeding from her. She held him to her even as her body lifted to each of his strokes into her pussy. And when he moved to the other breast to sample it, she cupped them both for him, and he fed from them back and forth as his cock felt ready to explode. Then, moving to her mouth, he kissed her.

She tasted of the way honey and flowers smelled in the spring. Her body felt like paradise and hell all at once. Paradise because of his need to keep her with him, and hell, because he knew that she'd leave him.

Rick fucked her harder now, feeling her body accepting his even as he lifted her ass up to pound her harder. When she tilted her head for him, he didn't ask her for permission, but licked the pounding pulse there and sank his fangs into her throat.

Her scream echoed in his head. She came three times as he drank from her, fucked her like a man possessed. And when his own climax raced over him, making his balls hurt just before they released, Rick felt her pull his wrist to her mouth, and she bit down just as he came the second time.

Darkness surrounded him in that moment, and he only just managed to hang onto consciousness. Nothing could have prepared him for the bond that held them as one. When he sealed the wound at her throat and took her again, marking her body with just a brush of his hand, Rick knew that she was his and would be for as long as she'd have him. Forever if she'd let him.

Everywhere he touched her, he could see his mark. She was his, his mind and body told him. This woman was his. And when she came again, this time wrapped around him like a glove, both her body and pussy, he came as well, filling her for the final time as he felt himself falling over the edge of darkness.

When he woke he was in his room on his bed, and not in the clinic where they had started out. Sitting up, he could see her at the window, one that had not been there before, with a sheet wrapped around her. When he said her name, she turned to him and he could see that she'd been crying.

"What is it? What's happened that has you upset like this?" Rick got up and went to her. Lifting her up and setting her on his lap, he held her as she sobbed against his chest, and tried to think how badly he'd hurt her when he'd taken her virginity. "I'm so very sorry, love. I should have been easier on you this first time. I promise you that a warm bath will help, and if you want, I can see about getting you some cream. I don't know if they make it, but I can find out."

She looked up at him. "You have not hurt me." He nodded and wiped at the tears on her cheek. "That was the most beautiful thing that has ever happened to me. And now you're going to think about what I am and who my sister is, and it will be gone. I don't have any desire to go back to her, so if you could find me a place to live here, I won't bother you again."

"No, the only place that you're going to live is here, with me." He held her and thought about her sister. He had no doubt that Lucia had sent her here to get him. For what, he could only guess, but Ryiah, as he'd been told, had only been the messenger, not the one that had hurt him. "You cannot leave me. And, to be honest, while I'm not sure how your sister came to hate me so much, I can tell you that you're not going to go back to her."

"Hunter told me that she was going to keep me from men my whole life. I know not why she'd do that to me. But she hates me more than you." He thought about what Nate had told him. "I shouldn't like to go to her again either."

"I'm going to tell you something that I only just found out. You're older than your sister." She looked up at him, and he could see the confusion on her face. "An hour older. I think that's the reason that she keeps you so close, so that no one will tell you. And the fact that without you finding your mate, she'd be able to rule you because your magic would never be fully realized."

"No, I'm the younger of us. It's why she's so powerful." He wasn't sure about that now but said nothing. When she sat up, he wanted to tell her he'd been joking and hold her again. The look on her face was full of hurt. "She said that I was hers to rule. That because I was younger that I would do as she said, and when she got the chance she would have someone murder me to take me out from under her care. I never understood her thinking on this, other than I must have done something to her long before I had any memories of it."

"I don't think that's right. I mean, her hatred of you, yes,

61

but not that she was stronger than you. She lied to you your whole life." He watched her face. When her eyes widened, he started to ask her what it was when he felt pain like he'd not felt in centuries. They were being marked.

Her body bowed from his and fell to the floor. As much as he wanted to go to her, he couldn't move over the pain in his own body. His back and legs felt like hot stakes were being burned against his flesh. His mouth shifted. His fangs felt like they were being pulled from his mouth. When he spit out the blood filling his mouth, his fangs were there as well, and he could feel new ones taking their place. Stronger and longer ones, he had no doubt. As he tried to hang onto consciousness, he reached for Ryiah.

Her screams hurt his head and his heart. Every time he touched her, just to brush his fingers over her skin, he knew that he was hurting her. But the need to hold her, bring her body to his, made him try and try again. When she curled into him, her body spooned to his, he knew a new kind of hell when he felt his back making room for what he could only assume were wings. It was too much. Rick just simply let the pain take him under.

The next time he woke he was in his bed again, but this time Ryiah was with him and curled around him. Holding her, he took an inventory of his body and knew that his legs were marked, as well as more of his back and chest. He could not imagine what was there, but knew that it would be part of the magic that came with being one of the warriors for Remy. A blood brother, as they'd been calling themselves.

When Ryiah lifted her head and looked at him, he told her he was sorry.

"I think we have been branded." He told her that was right, that it was from the magic here. He could see some smears on her face, but wasn't sure if it was just blood or actual tats. "Some. But there is also magic from you, as well as my own. I am...I was going to say that I am stronger, but I think that is a weak word for how I feel. I could easily take on someone much larger than me."

"You might have to." She said nothing, but laid her head back down while he explained about Benton and the malefactors, as well as the other things that had been going on since they started out. "As we gain our mates, we get stronger. So do our mates if they're not already fully charged up. But we haven't any idea what we are, where we're going from here, and how much magic we have. We sort of fumble into it as it happens."

"You can fly. I could before, but I think my wings are stronger for it. You have markings on you that are as ancient as I am, given to you by the queen of faeries, but also from magic that has been around for longer than even me." He asked her how she knew that. "I can read them. All of them. They're from my kind."

His body was hard with ideas. Not just that she could read the markings on him, but perhaps Remy and the others as well. When she looked down at him he could see that her throat was marked, and he was sure if he looked, her back and legs would be as well.

"When you say 'your kind,' what do you mean? Vicki, one of the other mates here, she's a faerie as well. But an earth faerie." She nodded and told him she could feel her. "And my tats, you can read them all? Not just the ones on my neck?"

When she touched her finger to the one that he'd had for a long time, he watched her face as she read what was there. "This man, Richard James, belongs to the queen of all faeries. To harm him is to harm me. When he is injured, all

63

who have caused him pain will die. Those that help him will be rewarded. Richard James belongs to me." She looked at him then. "Would you like to know what the rest of them say? They are spells mostly, but they list what you are and can do."

He nearly left the room, dragging her with him naked. Going back into their bedroom, he noticed in a vague sort of way that his bed was larger, his room as well. Where there was only the one window when he'd woken, he now had a wall of them. Even the ceiling was a large clear window. Rick thought that there was still a room about him—several, as a matter of fact—but as she needed light, the room had given it to her.

Once they were dressed, he kissed her again and grabbed her hand. It was time to talk to Remy and Skylar. They had to see if Ryiah could read them as well.

CHAPTER 4

Lucia was just leaving her chamber when pain took her to the floor. It wasn't until she tried to stand up that it literally took her breath away and had her curling into a ball to try to stem the hurt of it. She looked around for the source of it—someone was going to die for doing this to her—but she found herself alone. Not even a guard nearby to blame it on.

Her mind wasn't working well enough for her to think what had brought her to her knees, but she knew that whatever it had been, there would be hell to pay for it. And the fact that no one had come to see to her really pissed her off. When she could sit up she called for a guard, and when he was there, she killed him with her magic.

When the next one came in, she just stared at him from across the room. He was looking not at her but at the body of one of his cohorts, or whatever they called one another when they were alone. When she screamed, he looked up at her like he had no idea what he was doing there.

"If you don't get your ass over here and help me up, so help me I will hunt down every member of your family and kill them all slowly." That got him moving, but he didn't hold her so much as caused her more pain. But she was afraid to kill him just yet. If she did, he would surely drop her and she'd hurt more.

When she was in her bed, he asked her if she needed juice. A standard question, she supposed, but it still pissed her off. As she lifted her hands up to end him, he spoke quickly.

"Ryiah has made contact with the one you seek." She asked how he knew this. "I was with her when she encountered them. You sent me to make sure that she did her job. She has. I have no idea where she might be now. One of the women there picked her up from the arms of a man and flew away with her."

"What do you mean, flew away with her? Was she a faerie?" He said he did not think so. "Then how is it that she was able to fly? Only faeries can fly, and I did not allow any of them to be with her."

"But Hunter." She asked him what a hunter had to do with this. "The faerie that was with her. She is forever with her. I think you know her, my lady."

She did. That fucking little bitch that dared to turn her down when she told her she would come and be with her forever. Or until she tired of her, whichever came first. But to this man she was going to pretend that she meant little to her, and that she didn't know her.

"And why does she have a hunter with her?" He asked her what hunter. Lucia was beginning to think she was in a play, where everyone knew their lines but her. "Never mind. Find Ryiah and have her brought here. With the man she was to bring back to me. And while you're at it, find this Hunter. I want her to tell me why she thinks to leave this house without my permission. Does she not know that she belongs to me?"

"I know not what is in her mind, my lady." She wanted to snap his neck. When he started for the door, he paused and looked back at her. "My lady, you should be aware that there has been a great disturbance in the magic around this house. That was what caused my delay in coming to see you. The house is no longer protected by magic. And the people here, they are no longer yours to rule."

Long after he was gone, Lucia lay on the bed. Her mind was working on why the magic was no longer around the house and who she might have to kill to make sure that they left her magic alone. But in the back of her mind something kept tugging at her so that her sister was forefront several times in her thoughts. Lucia started to rise to check the books when she saw a faerie sitting at the foot of her bed.

"You wished to see me?" Lucia didn't care for her tone and snapped her fingers. Usually that would have them running, but this one just sat there. "My name is Hunter, in the event you'd ever bothered to know it. But we both know that you are aware of who I am, and also who I belong to."

"How dare you speak to me this way." She stood up and the faerie moved as well. She was just far enough away from her that Lucia couldn't grab her. "Where is she?"

"Who might you be talking about? There are a great many *shes* in this house. Or I should say, there *were* a great many in this house. There are only a few now. Male or female, as a matter of fact." Lucia asked her what she was talking about. "Shes. You asked me where she was. I'm telling you that I don't know which she you are talking about. There is you, of course, and me, but I don't think you would have said it that way if you meant me. Nor would you begin to ask me where you were. When you should...well, you might not know, but you might too. There is still Blue, but I think she was on her way out. And—"

"Shut up." Hunter only smiled at her. "Where is Ryiah? I've been told that you have been with her a great deal. I want you to tell me when to expect her back with my mate."

"Never." Lucia waited for more of an answer. When none seemed to be coming, she asked her again when she was returning. "When she has her powers sorted out, I would guess. And then there is the added magic that comes to her as well now. That's a lot of sorting out, don't you think?"

"She has no powers. And if you think to answer me in riddles again, I will have you killed." Hunter said nothing, but did smile bigger at her. "I hate you, Hunter. And would gladly kill you for this. What is it you think you know?"

"I know a great deal. Much more than you would wish the world to know about, I'm sure. Like that Ryiah is not just your sister, but older than you by fifty-nine and a half minutes. I know that you have lied to her all her life, keeping her under your thumb so that you could have her murdered." Lucia looked around for anyone that might have heard the little fucker. "And so you know, Richard wasn't your mate. He never was. We knew this, but let you believe it so you'd send her to the compound."

"Why would it be important for Ryiah to go to the compound?" She didn't think about the things Hunter had said to her. Didn't even want to know how she'd found out that Ryiah was her older sister, or how she'd been lying to her about their order of birth. But she really needed to know why it was important that Ryiah go there now. She was pretty sure she already knew that answer too.

"See? You do know it." When Hunter flew to the window and sat there, Lucia felt her knees weaken and slid to the floor rather than fall. "Does it bother you, Lucia, that your sister has finally found some happiness after living with you and being terrorized all her life? You're not nearly as stupid as we all think. Almost, but not nearly so. And yes, she's found her mate…the one we let you think was yours. We've been…all of us have been keeping him safe for her. Not you."

"She belongs to me. And so does he until I say differently. I shall say if she can have a mate or not." Hunter laughed, making the hair on the back of Lucia's neck dance with it. "Tell her to come here now. I wish to speak to her."

"No." Lucia looked at Hunter when she spoke. "I no longer serve you. None of us do, as a matter of fact. The only reason I'm here now is to distract you and to have a little fun while the rest of the inhabitants of your prison have time to gather what they can and leave."

"I won't allow that." Not that she could do much about it right now, but she was starting to see that things were going to go badly for her if she didn't regain some control over this. "You will not disobey me, Hunter. Go and find Ryiah and bring her to me this minute. I don't know where you heard those lies from, but they're not true. I am the eldest and I rule here."

"You only wish that you did. And as I have told you before, we know you not to be the oldest. Ryiah is. Whatever plans you had for her? They are now gone. She has come into her own." Hunter moved around the room again. This time when she landed, it was close enough for her to touch her should she want. Instead, she leaned back against the wall behind her and tried to think. Hunter continued as if she'd not just given her an order. "Her mate is a very powerful man. He has been touched by the queen. She had picked him for Ryiah long before you killed his family."

"Richard James." Hunter smiled. "No. He is my mate. I

will not have it. This was not in my plans, and I won't have you messing with them. Not to mention, had the queen picked him for my sister, I would have been informed of it. Someone would have told me."

"No, we would not have. It was fun having you believe that you were unable to kill him. You could not, but it was entertaining watching you think it was because he belonged to you. When all the time, your entire career of trying to end the James family for a thing that you did to yourself.... Well, it's given all of us a great laugh over the years." Lucia stood up, but the faerie did not move. "You can try to kill me, Lucia, but it won't work. I am no longer yours but belong to the true leader of our kind. Ryiah should have been the war queen long ago."

"We'll see about this." She went to the doorway and called to her guard. When no one came, not even her servants when she called for them, she turned back to Hunter. "They're out of the castle, I suppose. Trying to figure out why there is no magic around us to protect all that I own."

"You go on thinking that. But if I were you, I'd be trying to think of how to beg for mercy from Ryiah. She is not going to be happy to find out that you have lied to her over her lifetime, or to think of all the suffering she had to endure at your hand. Just to name a few, you put her in a dungeon for over two decades. Then you forced her hand when it came to protecting you from the Gathering. Not once, but several times. And know this...when they find out what you did to her, they won't be angry at her, but you. You did this all to yourself, and now you have to pay the price for it." Lucia did remember that. And a great deal more things she'd done and said to her sister. In that moment, she was suddenly afraid of Ryiah. "I would be as well should I have the list of things against me that you have."

"She's my sister. She cannot harm me." Hunter said nothing. "You know this as well as I. She cannot harm me any more than I could have her. And I did try."

"So you did. But you are forgetting that you harmed her by lies and deceit. You gained by harming her. You profited off her blood. And you did this with the full knowledge that she was greater than you." Hunter flew off the bed and moved out her chamber door. "I only came by to tell you that she shall not be returning. None of us will, as a matter of fact. Ryiah won't, at least not in the capacity that she had been before. All that you own is hers now, and rightfully so. So with that being said, I will take my leave of you. Goodbye, Lucia. I would like to say it has been a pleasure, but it hasn't. You're a mean, spiteful faerie that is going to get all you deserve."

After she was gone, Lucia tried to think. If Ryiah had her power, of which there was no doubt of that now, then she could easily destroy her. Not just kill—that would be too easy—but to literally destroy her, make her suffer in ways that would last lifetimes. She would also command the faeries. Lucia had figured out over the years that not only were they small, but they were vicious as well when they felt they'd been slighted in some way. And the pain they would inflict would be more than anyone had ever felt before. She knew as surely as she was standing there that they'd be particularly horrible to her. All because she told Ryiah a few lies and seen that a few of the faeries were killed.

As she moved through the house to find someone to help her, she noticed the changes. Gone was the chair that she'd spent so much time in. Now it was only the plastic one that she'd formed it from. The walls that had looked like they had been papered in cloth, their print so fresh all the time that it looked like art rather than just a simple covering, were gone as well. In their place were dried dirty walls that sagged badly. There were also piles of trash, more than likely the same ones that had been in this house when she came to it. Instead of cleaning it as she should have, she'd covered everything in magic. And why not? She'd had an abundance of it.

The drapes that she had agonized over for days were now just rags hanging over the filthy windows. Again, just like they had been when she'd entered this house all those years ago. The floors, for all the beautiful tile, was now dirt and stone. Lucia had to step carefully so as not to fall to the sublevels below, it was so bad. Furniture was gone, with not even a faded place in the dirt to show that anything had been there. The windows that had not been covered were broken, their beauty now lost because the magic was leaving her. Stepping into her office, a place that she'd spent countless hours going over each plan and every coin that she'd been able to gather, she saw that it was in ruin as well. The fireplace grate was broken, with large pieces of the stone inside of it. It had never occurred to her that the house would continue to decay around her magic. Not that she would have given it any thought at the time, but now it was terribly sad. The room also had a chill. Lucia was sure the reason for that was that she'd spent so much time in here making her sister heel to her.

Lucia was going to have to do something, and soon. Ryiah could not treat her this way. She would have to give her back all her things, all the magic that had been hers. When someone laughed in the room, Lucia looked around twice before she realized she was alone. When they laughed again, she crawled under the table and hid. There was no magic anymore to keep the monsters at bay.

~~~

Master moved along the streets. There were no humans around that he could bring to his work area to help him with his cause. He was going to need them, and he had a feeling that Rembrandt was keeping them away from him. Twice he'd thought he'd seen someone, but they were gone before he could make his big body go in that direction. Things were falling off him daily now. He'd lost one of his fingers just this morning.

"Rembrandt has much to pay for." His mind was slightly fuzzy on the reason it was Rembrandt's fault for his pain and suffering. Even he at times wondered who the man was or how they were connected, but figured that there were just too many times when the man's name would come up when he had something go wrong. He had to be guilty for most of it. "And that woman of his. She has white burning magic that has hurt me on more than one occasion."

That wasn't right either. There were two women, and they both had hurt him. One of them had gunned him down, using a weapon like none he'd ever seen. But the one with the white fingers, she had burned into his flesh so deeply that he had not been able to heal from it. He looked down at the festering wound and knew that he'd have to do something about it soon. It was smelling again.

Twice now he'd had to lie down and wait for the pain to go away. He was also easily exhausted, almost to the point of passing out from it. And both times after sitting down, when he'd risen up he'd nearly gagged from the odor coming from him. Just a few days ago he'd sewn it shut, only to have it seep green, vile-smelling stuff until he had to tear his stitches out again. Then there were the things that went on in his head.

Odd thoughts were there, not just on the things he needed to get done, but he was sure that he had a bug that lived in his brain telling him things to do and how to do them. It hurt at times, but he could feel it moving, like it was setting up furniture. It played loud music too.

"You are by far one of the stupidest creatures I have ever had the misfortune to meet. You have no bug in your head. You're crazy, that's all." Mary again. Every time he thought her gone, she'd come back to make him want to cry like a small baby. "When are you going to listen to me and realize that the only reason you can hear me is because you bring me about? I'm dead. So are Dolin and Ward."

"Nay, I spoke with Dolin just this morning. He told me to get out and walk about in the sun. It would make me feel better." She told him that was her. "I think I would know the voice of my best friend. You are not. I don't like you at all."

"Dolin is not your best friend. He used you as he did everyone else. You hated him. As for me, you did, at one time, like me. You loved me as much as Dolin and Ward did. You're just upset that you killed us all and are left alone." He told her that he'd not killed her. "You might as well have. Were you not the reason that I was at the compound in the first place? Had you done what you were told and when you were told, I would be alive. As would *my* dear friends, Dolin and Ward. You were slow to act and got us all killed. We'd all be rich and you'd be working for Dolin and Ward. Even me. But we're dead and you're stupid."

"I am not stupid. Stop saying that to me. I would rule this world...Dolin and Ward both told me I would." She called him a liar. "I am nothing of the kind. I will rule here."

"Not with Remy and his bitch of a mate hanging around, you won't. How long do you think it will be before they come across the body parts that you're leaving behind to figure out where you've gone? A week? Perhaps only a few days?

I think within the hour they will come upon your scales and pick them up, until they come upon a great deal of them in the form of you." He told her to leave him alone. "For me to do that, you must stop thinking about me, you moron."

Tuning her out as he turned to go down the next street, he wondered why anyone would want the sun to beat down on them when it was so cold otherwise. It was then that he saw the house. It took him several moments to realize that it seemed to be falling in on itself. Very quickly. Lifting his good arm up, he rubbed his eyes and looked again. The roof had fallen in on one side, and the grass seemed to have grown a near foot in that short amount of time he'd taken to rub his eyes. He started forward when Ward told him to wait.

"It might harm you if you venture too far. And I think you are hurt enough without going to look for trouble, don't you?" He agreed with him and told him thank you. "I was thinking that you should sit back and wait to see what trickery this is. Whatever is in there, it might come out and help you. Or it could harm you greatly."

"You mean the magical being that lives there? You think it might have information on how to get me more drugs?" Ward told him anything was possible. "I would very much like to not hurt anymore, Ward. I think I have suffered greatly and there is no reason for it. I have begged and begged Rembrandt to come to me so that I might kill him, and still he keeps me from my needs. It is most unfair of him."

"I think so as well. He's much like Hector. There was no reason for him to allow Rembrandt to kill our Mary, yet he did nothing but watch as she was murdered like she meant nothing to us. I think he needs to die as well." There was something there, a pain of some memory, but it was gone before he could catch it enough to think on it. "You think too hard, Benton.

Maybe you should just let us think for you."

"Yes, yes. I like that idea. It pains my head too much to think anyway. You tell me what to do and I shall not think. That doesn't mean that you're in charge. No, that would be me. But for now, you can think for me." He sat down, his big body just too much to move any more. "I am falling apart, Ward. Just losing bits and pieces of me more and more every day. Whatever shall I do about it?"

"There, did you see it? The way the house moved just now?" He looked at the house as Ward continued. "You are falling apart but you still have a brilliant mind. If you could only get someone to help you, all would be well. Perhaps the answer is there, in that house of magic."

The house was falling down now. There had been a pretty garden out front, but now it was all weeds. The chimney was smoking for a bit, but soon it was nothing but a pile of rubble as well. He spied a human, one that came out to see the magic disappear, he supposed, but Master was just too exhausted to go and get her. She would have to wait until later for him to give her the pleasure of making her his slave.

So many had begged him to be his workers. They were never as good as the first few, but they had tried. And when it had come time to let them go, he did.... There was a store not far from here, he remembered, and they'd had many bottles of drugs. He wondered if he took the human there, if she would be able to get him something for his pain. Master looked at his arm that was now hanging limply at his side.

"Whatever happened to me?" He wanted to cry at all the wounds he had. "Someone has taken to hurting me when I rest. Or when one of the dark times takes me." He tried to remember why he was sitting on the cold ground when he looked at the house. It seemed to be falling apart right before his very eyes. "Do you think the house is tired?"

His giggle startled him, and he looked around to see if anyone had heard him. Superior men such as himself did not giggle like small children. But he looked at the house again, and there was a human there. He wondered what she was looking at and turned in that direction. There was a house there that was falling apart.

"Focus." He felt his body cringe from the harshness of Mary's voice. "You are looping around over and over the same thoughts and giving me a head pain. The house you have looked at several times. The woman as well. She is not going to help you; you are scaring her. Now. I want you to focus on the house and tell me what you see there."

"If you wish to live in it, my dear, I think you can do better. It is nothing but a shack. Nothing to concern yourself with." She told him to keep looking at it. "I am. There is nothing going on there but a woman screaming at the house, and she is.... I have never seen her before, have I?"

"No, you have not. What is she saying? Why would someone scream at a house?" He said he didn't know but stood to get closer. It pained him so much to move after sitting for so long, and he nearly went back to the ground. But he would do this for Mary because she was his one and true love. "No, I am not. I don't even like you very much. Most of the time not at all."

"You jest. I know that you are in love with me." She told him that she hated him at this moment. "I should like for you to bring our children to see me soon. The girls must be so grown by now. And our son is going to be a great deal like me, I think. I know that they will be afraid of me, but I shall cover up the bad parts and just watch them."

"You have no children, Benton. And I am not your wife.

You're thinking of Rembrandt's wife and his children again. You remember them. They're the ones that you had murdered. I was in love with Ward and Dolin until Rembrandt took my still-beating heart from my chest. He murdered me. And for what good reason?" He told her he was sorry for her loss. "Thank you. Someday you will have to bring me flowers. Just to put on the little plot of land that was built for me."

"You are here? In the ground?" She told him that she was on the other realm. "I cannot go back there, Mary. You know that. Rembrandt closed it off to me. I must stay here where I cannot get the medications that I so need."

"He is a monster. So are you, but he is cruel in his treatment of all of us. I suppose you are as well. The way you've hurt every creature you've ever come across just because you could." He grinned at the memory, then frowned. He wasn't sure what he was supposed to be doing again. "The woman."

"Yes, the woman. She had white fingers that burned into me." He looked in the direction of where the store he'd been thinking about had been. The one that had some drugs in it.

"Not her, you fool. The one at the falling down house. She's there, screaming at the house. Look." He did and saw no one, and asked Mary about it. "Of course, there is no one there now. Had you done something, like to go and see what she was about, you would have had her. Damn it, Benton, you let her get away. But I suppose Rembrandt is responsible for that too. I tell you, Benton, that man has a great many things to be punished for. It's too bad that you cannot read or write. You could have been making a list about these things and told him of them as you made him suffer."

Master didn't even bother telling her that he had more important things to do than to learn his letters and numbers. Someone, long ago, had tried to teach them to him, but his head was fuzzy again and he couldn't place it. His wife? No, Mary had said that he'd not been married. But then who?

He made his way back to his cave. He'd tried living in a house, a grand house, but he could never remember where it was when he left it. Then there was the damage that kept happening to it when he was there. This was something else that he wanted to blame on Rembrandt, but he could not. Master was just too big, he supposed, and looked down at his body.

Most of the scales on his limp arm were gone. The rest of his body was in poor shape as well. But dragging his arm along behind him had done most of that. His fingers were forever getting caught up in things, and broken off as well. His belly had a large hole in it, and no matter how much he tried to heal it with magic or some of the other things he'd found around, it still smelled and seeped. Even when he'd tried sewing it shut, he'd had problems. He looked at what was left of his tail.

Several days ago he'd been walking along when he'd fallen. He could not remember why. Things for the most part were all messy in his head. But when he woke from a dark time, he had no tail and his body was covered in blood. It wasn't until just yesterday that he'd found it lying outside his cave. He was sure that Rembrandt had snuck into his dwelling and chopped it off him. Master had no excuse for the blood, but figured that Rembrandt had done that as well.

"The bastard." He did wish now that he'd let Rembrandt's lovely wife, Shandell, show him his letters. She'd been a good woman. He wondered what had happened to her and their three children. When Mary told him that was Rembrandt's wife, not his, he wanted to deny it, but he then remembered the poor woman's burnt body on the ground and thought Mary to be telling him no falsehood. Curling around the fire that he'd started, Master thought of his plans for Rembrandt when he came to him.

"He will die slowly. And when he is gone, I shall rule this realm and all that live here. I will be a true master of all that I can see. Rembrandt will be my biggest prize." Mary told him that wasn't going to work if Rembrandt was dead. "Leave me in peace, woman. I have thinking to do."

But before he could focus his mind on anything, exhaustion took him and he closed his eyes. He would think on the morrow, when his head was clear and the pain in his body was no longer making him ill.

CHAPTER 5

Each of them stared at her. Vicki was sure that they were trying not to, but even she felt her eyes drift to her over and over. The meeting wasn't going well anyway, but this was just too much to let go. She stood up when Remy asked if there was anything else.

"She's a faerie. Not like me, but more." The woman, Ryiah, stood up as well. "What are you? I know that you're Rick's mate. Hell, we all felt the earth move when he claimed you. But you aren't human. What are you other than faerie?"

"I don't know." Vicki didn't know if she believed her or not. "My sister.... She was once a war faerie. But now, I'm not sure what she is other than a tyrant and a horrible person. I have only just found out that I am the elder of the two of us, and that all this time she has lied to me. I know not why she did that either."

"I do." Everyone turned to look at the pretty little faerie that had come in when Rick and Ryiah had. "Ryiah is a true war faerie, and she has been one since birth. Had her father been home at the time of her birthing, he would have known who she was and marked her as the one he would train when she was old enough. But their mother, a meaner woman you do not want to know, lied for her own gain and told everyone that Lucia was the one who should be the daughter who stood alongside her father. I heard that Lucia had been easy to manipulate, but now I'm not so sure. I think her much like her mother, if not worse."

"I don't understand. You mean only the oldest girl can be a war faerie?" Hunter told her the oldest child only could claim the rights of this birthright. "So it matters little if they are girl or boy? So long as they're firstborn? Good. I like that. But how could he have not known who was the true fighter?"

"He did, eventually. When Lucia's skills as a fighter were less than perfect, a thing that a firstborn would know from their first breath, he washed his hands of her. I don't know if he ever tried to figure out what had happened. This was before I was born to Ryiah. But that did not stop her mother from finding every way possible for her daughter Lucia to be the best, or give the appearance of being the best. But it was all magic, something that even now Lucia has very little of. She even went so far as to begin killing those that knew the truth or might have guessed it."

"Where is she now? The mom? Maybe she can help us out on why this was done. And short of that, we can beat it out of her." Hunter told Skylar that she was dead. "I'm sorry."

"Lucia had her killed." Ryiah got up to pace and Vicki watched Rick. For a man that had professed no need of a mate and that he wanted little to do with one, he was looking at Ryiah like she meant the world to him. Vicki looked at Ryiah when she started talking again. "I have been a slave to Lucia since the day after I changed. The change in us occurs when we are thirteen. It's then that our bodies become magical. We come into our own, I guess you could say. I remember my time like it was only a few days ago. The feeling of power had washed over me and I was marked. My wings came then as well. But later in the day, after I was told to rest even though I felt wonderful, my mother told me that Lucia had evolved as well. That because she was the oldest that it had been harder on her. That the magic she got was so powerful that it took her under. I have since figured out it was a way for Lucia to watch the changes in me so that she could mimic them later when Mother freed her from her rest. I hate to believe that even my mother was a part of this, but I think it's true as well."

"So you believed them even then. But what of the timing of the event? I mean, you did it first, correct?" Vicki had wanted to ask the same thing and was glad that Rick had. "I mean, as the firstborn, you had your evolving first, right? Did you believe even then that your sister had gotten more?"

"I had no reason not to believe them when they said it. And when she came from our room a few days later, she told me that she had wrapped her magic around her in a way that no one would see her markings until she wanted them to. She thought it would keep her safe, she said. I never found out what she was keeping herself safe from, but as I said, I had no reason not to believe what she said to me. I was in awe of her, I think. But then the trouble began for me."

Vicki knew that when she'd arrived she'd been hurt. Before she could ask her what sort of trouble there had been, Hunter began speaking.

"They knew…the faeries of her father had figured out that they had been switched at birth, or that their order of birth was wrong. By the time they had proof of it, her father had been murdered. I believe, as do a great many others, that Lucia had done the same to him as she did later to her mother.

Turned them into the Council for crimes that she herself had committed. And since she was nothing more than a child, not even fourteen or so at the time, they had no reason to think she'd lie to them. After the trial and eventual beheading of both their mother and father, we were going to confront the queen when she came to us.

"The woman who marked me." Rick stood up then, and Vicki noticed something that she hadn't before. Rick was bigger. Not just in muscle, but he was taller too. She thought him to be at least several inches taller than he'd been before. "I was at the home of my brother, the day after my sister-in-law had been killed, when she came to me. She marked me and told me that I was going to have a lot of things happen to me, as well as a lot of death. But that this woman would come for me that she'd been saving for me. I just found out that it was Ryiah."

"Has she returned to you as yet?" Hunter flew around the room back and forth, like she was pacing, but in the air. When no one answered her, she looked at Remy and asked him if he'd seen her.

"I have not, I don't believe. Would I know her should she come to me?" Hunter told him he'd never doubt it if she came to him. "Then no, I have not seen her. But I do have a couple of questions. Rick said that Ryiah can read our markings. I should like very much for her to see if she can tell us what some of these marks say. It might help us in ridding the world of Benton and the malefactors. Also, you said you were born of Ryiah. I would like to know what you meant by that as well."

"When I was locked away, a seed floated on the air to me. I wasn't sure what it meant. There were no windows where I was locked away and no soil for me to think that it came from the earth. It was just there." Ryiah put out her hand and smiled when the little faerie landed on it. "I had only to capture it in my palm, and when I held it, I could feel her warmth, even her heart beating against my skin. After a few days, no more than two I think, I opened my palm and there she was. My best and only friend. And over the next decades she and others would somehow come into my hole and bring me food and treats. As well as a little soil in their pockets. It was enough, after a time, that I could feed from it. They saved me."

No one said anything, but Vicki could see their sorrow, feel it even. How could anyone treat a person this way? And it being their sister? When Hunter moved to Ryiah, Vicki could see their friendship, love even, and knew in that moment that Hunter had not just saved Ryiah, but she was pretty sure that they'd saved each other. Ryiah cleared her throat when Hunter moved to her shoulder.

"I would need to touch you." Vicki, like the rest of them, turned to look at Skylar. She wasn't normally possessive, not like Remy could be, but Vicki had a feeling that when Ryiah had said she had to touch Remy, it wasn't going to be a simple touch. "He would need to be exposed to me as well."

Skylar looked amused. So when she nodded, Ryiah put her hands behind her back and asked again if she could touch her mate. "You only need to touch him, not have sex with him, correct?"

"Nay, I should not like to have sex with him at all. It is most.... I have had it today, and while I need Rick again, I don't think I should like to go that far with your mate." Everyone laughed, but Vicki could see that Ryiah was confused. "If you would be so kind, sir, as to remove your shirt. I will tell you what it says."

"Wait." Ruben left them then but returned shortly with

his camera, as well as a recorder that he'd been using. "I can remember a great deal, but I don't want to miss details. If you can tell me what some of the markings mean, I'd like to compare them to other things I have found. Like the markings on the earth to protect us. And the ones on the windows of some of the stores that we're now using."

Ryiah stepped forward and Rick stood behind her. He didn't touch her, even though she could almost feel that he wanted to, but stood there while she put her fingers on the first line of markings on Remy.

"Rembrandt, a man of war and a man of all men. The rest is about your wife and children, how they died and you mourned them. Shall I read it or go on?" He told her to go on please. "There is a list of things you can do. Flying is first. Then there is mention of your body art. It says that you have been equipped with a claymore sword as well as numerous knives. You have an endless supply of stars to throw, as well as ammo for your guns."

"Stars?" Vicki moved closer when Skylar did. "You mean this? I thought those were just.... Remy, look. You have silver stars at the base of your head that you can pull away."

Two were taken from his neck and he tossed them across the room. When they stuck into the wall, it took a great deal of power to remove them. Vicki found some on her own body, as well as Davis's. She wondered how long they'd been there.

There were other weapons as well, most they knew of. In addition to the wings, there was body armor. And once he was told how to activate it, they all played with the one that seemed to come with their bodies as well. Vicki thought of all the times this might have come in handy.

"All right, so now we have a better supply of weaponry. Can you tell me what we are?" Ryiah looked around the room, then back at Remy again. "You do know, don't you? You know just what we all are."

"Yes. You are a warrior. Not faerie nor fae, but all of them. Stronger than most anything that I have ever met, yet you are gentle when necessary. Davis is the same, not as strong but a great warrior too. As is Vicki." She looked at Leo and Jamey. "Dragons that are stronger than any I have ever encountered, and you have shared this strength with the rest. You can come together should you need the extra magic, or you can fight independently should that be necessary as well. Children of you both, should you desire to have them, would have the same ability. And when they find mates, they too will be given this great gift. Also, you would only need to think of battle armor when you are your other halves. Then it will cover you. From your head to the tip of your tail, you will be encased in a magic that will protect you from anything. Even now you can protect your human part by doing the same."

They did it, both of them covered in the same armor that Vicki and the others had. Their faces were open, but she could feel the protection of something around her cheeks and nose. Even her eyes, usually so exposed when blood was splashing around, seemed to be covered.

Ryiah turned to Chris then. "The cat that the two of you can become, as well as all the other animals, are all under the same protection. Once you have come together, I'm sure that you have noticed that you're larger. That is due to the armor as well. But all of you carry a mark that hides you away. The shield that hides your true self from humans keeps you from being a target. They would not understand seeing a cat as large as the one you are, so if you have changed, they see only what is necessary so that they don't run screaming from you. Some will see a small house cat; others will see a panther.

Your enemies will see what you are, a great monster of a cat that will kill them." Chris held onto Kate as Ryiah looked at Remy again. "The markings on your body are all made from a language that has not been spoken for many decades. I speak it because I have talked to the others for as long as I can remember. The other faerie as well as fae. They are my friends."

"We are your army, my lady." Ryiah asked Hunter what she meant. "When your father was killed, everyone knew who you were. Even wondered for a while when you were going to come for them. But then they saw what was going on and protected you as best we could. Even when you were locked away, as you said, we brought you things, food, and drink to keep you from being too weak. And when you were well, you came out to the grounds and spoke to us. There were many that said they only stayed because of you. Now all of them know why they were drawn to the woods around the house. It was to be there for you when you called us to arms."

"But I have no use for an army. I would not even know how to command one." Hunter nodded and landed on her arm. Vicki, like the rest of them, watched as the mark that hadn't been there before bled through her skin and showed itself. It was a sword with a crest on it. Ryiah ran her finger over the marking and when she spoke, there was such emotion in her voice.

"It's my father's. He carried it to battle every day of my young life." Hunter told her to bring it forth. When it peeled from her body, they all stepped back. It was large, sharp, and made of a material so brilliant that Vicki was sure that it was covered in magic. "When he was taken before the Gathering, they asked him for it but no one seemed to know where it was. Even mother didn't know other than the fact that he'd carried it with him all the time. My father said not a word about it. Do you suppose he knew where it was?"

"He willed it to you, my lady. It has been there all this time, waiting for you to be able to bring it forth without Lucia trying to take it from you. And she would have. Not that it would have worked for her. Your father knew even then that there had been a mistake. And since you are the true faerie warrior, you will have all of us at your call." Ryiah shook her head, but Hunter nodded. "It is the way of our kind. You are now the ruler of one of the greatest armies of all time."

~~~

Rick watched Ryiah. They'd gone back to their room over an hour ago and he'd been afraid to touch her. She still held her father's sword, hers now, he supposed, in her hand. He knew that she couldn't harm him, but accidents could happen and she was stressing enough without adding him being stupid and getting hurt to the list. He wanted to ask her what else she'd come across in reading the marks on their bodies and if she knew how to use them. Remy and Skylar were out now playing with the ones she had read of theirs, and having a grand time of it.

"Do you have a mark as well?" Rick told her that he did, in the same place as hers. "My mother didn't. I'm not sure why, but she didn't. At least, I never saw it. And had she had one, I'm sure she would have been showing everyone."

"Hunter said that the sword would have come to you, but the fact that you could take it out to use means that it feels you're worthy of it and safe. Perhaps it didn't think your mother was." Ryiah snorted. "Were you mistreated by her as well?"

"In an indirect way, I guess. She would have others say things to me, get them to harm me. Mostly it was through

89

Lucia." Ryiah turned and looked at him. "Hunter told me that I have an army larger than my father's was. That there are more faeries willing to come and help me than she'd ever seen."

"Before she came to talk to you, she told us how you would sit at the woods and give them treats. That you'd warn them when Lucia was coming for them. You even devised a way for them to get out of the house before you came here." Ryiah nodded. "Did you really think that you would be killed coming here?"

"I did. I even hoped for it. She'd sent a few people to come for you before it occurred to her that I might die when I did it. When she was told that they couldn't cross over the barrier with the idea to kidnap you, she told them to simply not think about it. Like that was supposed to work. Twice that I'm aware of the people simply stopped coming back. I believe they're here. Where they can be safe." He nodded, thinking that she more than likely had told them to do that. "What happens now?"

"What do you mean?" She told him her thoughts. "You and I are a couple. And you stay here with me. Unless you wish to move elsewhere. But wherever you go, that's where I'll go as well."

"Chris and Kate are going to live among the humans for a few weeks at a time. Can you tell me why?"

"Yes. Remy wanted to make sure that when this is over with Benton and the monsters, we can slide into living with people again without standing out. It's also a way to see if we can be out there being as marked up as we are. But I guess you cleared that up for us now, so I'm not sure what will happen. I believe that they have already purchased a home and are currently moving things into it." She nodded. "Would you like to do that as well?"

"No. I don't care for people for the most part. I mean, I can get along with them, but I'm not terribly trusting. I don't have a real skill other than to be afraid all the time." He thought that wasn't quite true but said nothing as she continued. "You've taken my blood. I mean, I have yours as well. But it doesn't seem to have any ill effects on you. I mean, as you have pointed out, I'm a faerie and you're a vampire."

"I actually thought of that while we were in the shower this morning. Drinking from a faerie should make me nuts. At least a little nuttier than I am usually. But while I can feel the power of it, the way it makes me feel like I can lift buildings, I don't feel as if I have to drain you every time I'm close to you. I do, however, want to lay you out and feast on some of your other very tasty parts."

"I'd like that as well." She lay back on the bed and he stood up. "Did you know that we can be naked should we want? With just a thought?"

He had, but when she was naked for him, like she was now, all he could think about was how much of her he wanted to taste. How he'd like nothing better than to start at one end of her and not stop until he was at the other, tasting and touching every part of her as he went.

Dropping to his knees where her hips were just hanging over the bed, he touched his fingers to her flesh just above the juncture at her thighs.

"I can taste the difference in your skin when you're aroused. Like right now, if I were to bite you here I know that the blood would be hot, spiced just enough for me to get a buzz from it, because you're ready for me." He kissed the area before moving to the pulse at her thigh. "Here I know that I could feed well. The blood would be hotter still, taste like you're ready to come, and when you do, I will be able to not just smell you, but I could actually taste where your body gives off the endorphins that taste only of you."

"Touch me again, Rick." He did so now, kissing her first then sinking his fangs into the warm vein that lay just at the surface of her skin. When she cried out, he slid his finger into her sheath and fucked her slowly as he drank deeply from her. And when she came again, he tasted her pussy with his tongue after sealing the small wounds.

She rode his mouth, giving him so much of her cream that he knew that no matter how fast he drank from her, he was missing a great deal. And when she came a third and fourth time, he lifted his head up but continued fucking her with his fingers. She was beautiful. A tame word, he thought, but that was all he could think of at the moment.

Willing his clothing away, he wrapped his hand tightly around his cock and fisted himself while he watched her. He thought her to have the most perfect body he'd ever had the pleasure of seeing. And it was all his.

"Come here to me, Rick. I want to ride your cock." He moved to the bed, making sure to lick any part of her that he could reach. Her nipples, her navel. He even touched his tongue to her hip and ribs. Nothing about her was off-limits, and when he lay back on the bed, he held his cock in his hand while she slid down over him. The look of pleasure on her face was nearly his undoing. He rose up into her twice before she told him to be still.

"What do I do? I have thought of nothing but having your cock inside of me for hours, but I don't know what to do now." He put his hands on her hips and rolled her forward slightly. "Oh yes. More of that. I love the way you feel. So deep and hard."

He let her pick the pace, but feeling her slowly ride him was almost as painful as it was when she slid over him fast. Each time that she was close to coming she'd stop, holding herself as still as she could while her body milked him. As her juices ran down his body and over his balls, Rick had to grab the sheets so as not to flip her to her back and take her hard enough to empty himself deep within her.

Her hands were on her breasts, pulling and pinching her nipples. Then she would tug at his, nearly making him beg her to finish him. When she leaned down, crying out when she came, in her excitement she bit down hard on his nipple and drew blood. Rick held her there while she fed from him, lifting his hips up to fuck her while she did so.

"Take me."

He didn't have to be told twice. Rolling her to her back, her legs wrapped around his waist, Rick fucked her as hard as he could, pounding her hard enough to move her up over the bed until he had to hold her there. When he was close, feeling his impending climax roll over him, he leaned into her throat and bit down. His release had him howling against her skin, the power of it nearly making him black out as everything he had seemed to spill from his cock into her.

Blood flooded his mouth, spilling over his lips and making him swallow twice as he felt his body ready for a second powerful climax. Lifting her to him by cupping her firm ass, holding her body as close to him as he could, he begged her to bite him and offered his throat. But instead of biting him there, she slashed her hand over his heart and laid her mouth over the open wound. This type of bonding, he knew, was what changed humans to vampires, and he wondered briefly what it would do to her, if anything. Rick took her wrist to his mouth and bit down on her even as his climax took him under.

He woke only seconds later, her body still beneath his, and Rick rolled to his back, taking her with him until he could catch his breath. When he was able to, a good ten minutes had passed and he sat on the side of the bed and stretched out his beaten muscles. Christ, if they kept this up, he'd be dead within a week. Going to the bathroom, leaving her to rest, he looked in the mirror at the man staring back at him.

He'd been tatted before she'd come into his life, but he could see that he'd had more art added in the last few hours. In addition to the sword that had been on his forearm, there were more glyphs than there had been, as well as a few words that had been added to the one at his throat. He could read them now. Not just the old language, but he could also make out the drawings and what they meant as well. He was staring at one particular sentence when Remy touched his mind.

The marking that I have on my chest, the one that you said was a dragon, did you know what it meant when you said I could call it to me? He told him no, he'd only been able to tell him what it said. *Well, you should come and see what I've discovered. Or what we've discovered. I'm telling you, Rick, that someday I'm going to look at this and go, yes, I know just what that means. I don't think I've ever been so frustrated in my life.*

You're sounding a little like that now. Leaving the bathroom, he looked down at Ryiah as she slept. *Do you suppose that when she calls to the army, as Hunter said she could, we can defeat Benton once and for all?*

I've been thinking on that as well. And I've a feeling that we cannot do that, defeat him that is, until we are twelve. He asked him what he meant. *I think we're only biding our time, getting more and more powerful all the time, until Nate's love gets here. I've a feeling, as does my Skylar, that we're going to be at our best when she gets here. I can only imagine what she'll bring to our brotherhood.*

For some reason Rick didn't think it would be that easy. That even as strong as they'd be at twelve, Benton would still be something hard to bring down. Even as beaten as he was, they still hadn't been able to kill the monster. They'd been trying for a long time and had only, in all this time, managed to hurt him off and on. Things had to change soon. Rick wanted to play at being a mate to his faerie.

Letting Ryiah sleep, he went to find Remy and the others. He was both surprised and pleased to see Nate there. He was getting…well, stronger might be the wrong word to use with him, but he was getting better. Rick hoped that when his mate did come to him that she wasn't going to be afraid of the big man.

CHAPTER 6

Benton buried his tail and decided at that moment that he was going to go and kill Rembrandt. He'd been fooling with him long enough. Pulling his shovel out of the soil, he watched as the ground bubbled up first, then spit out the acidic liquid that had been leaking out of the end of the tail when he'd brought it here. Then he watched as the dirt surrounding the grave blackened and burned, as if poison had been put in it.

"Serves you right for what you've done to me. And should you wish to blame someone, 'tis not me. I have nothing to do with this poison you have. You must blame Rembrandt and those men of his. They're the ones that never listen to me and die. What should you do if I were to plant his dead body into your belly?" He thought it more than likely the soil would grow strong trees and pretty flowers. "You would to, wouldn't you?"

As he made his way back to his cave, he could feel his body getting stronger. He wasn't sure what it was that had brought about this change, but he was going to make plans and carry them out. It was time for this to end. As he put his things away, having cleaned his entire cave well this morning, he looked around his dwelling and smiled.

"'Tis fit for a king, I think."

He'd tried living in the houses below, the large buildings that had so many nice things in them that he wanted to own them all. But his size and his body had kept him from entering the dwellings, both taking out walls and collapsing floors. In one home he'd even fallen through the yard and into a kind of sublevel compartment. He'd been so angry about someone hiding things from him that he'd destroyed the house as well as the three on either side of it. That was when he found the box.

At first his only thought was to toss it aside. But when it rattled, much like his medicine box had when Randall had shown him the wonders of the drugs that he'd drank, he decided to see what it was about. Picking it up carefully the second time, he opened it up and found all sorts of wonders. But the stones had startled him.

There were perhaps fifty of them, all in different colors and sizes. Most were as big as his palm, their richness so wonderful that he'd nearly taken them all to the chamber in his heart. The few that were smaller, but not by much, were plentiful too. Setting it aside, as one would a great treasure, he began looking for other such boxes of stones.

The house was filled with them. Some of them were behind glass that had light shining over them. Some had been made into things to wear. He had no idea why someone would do such a thing to something so precious, but he laid them with the others, putting them down and arranging them until he had them just right. But he found more and more as he began to search, and when he'd exhausted what was there, he moved to the next house, then the next. That was when he came upon a large building that looked much like the lab in the other realm.

He couldn't read. He had an idea that someone had tried to show him his letters long ago, but that memory, like a great deal of other things in his head, was muddled around. But he found papers that had pictures of the stones that he wanted. When he made his way into the big building, being careful where he walked, he found more stones than he'd ever seen in all his life. And not just the magical ones that would serve him, but brightly colored ones that were all the colors of the earth as well. And they were displayed as if they knew he was coming. Someone, he thought, knew how to treat a man such as himself.

It had taken him the better part of the day to gather them all. Some of them had been crushed in his haste to get them all, but he knew that even the dust of them could bring him such happiness. Getting things to carry them in with his one good arm had been difficult as well, but he managed. And when he'd come across some bags made of some material that he'd never encountered before, he was able to load a great many of them into these and hang them from his spikes at his back and what was left of his tail. Taking them back to his dwelling, he had laid all the bags in a neat row and looked around. The place hadn't been fit for such a man, he'd thought.

He'd been living in a dump. Master had decided that the mess did not suit his newfound wealth either, and he began piling the trash that he'd just tossed anywhere into the pit he'd been using as a fire. Setting a flame to it, he'd been so warm for the first time in weeks that he'd had to leave his home for a few moments to cool down. That, too, was so gratifying, beginning to feel so alive.

When he'd had it cleaned to his standards, hating that

he'd had to do it all on his own but loving that he was getting somewhere, Master sat down and looked at the bounty that he'd found. And there was so much of it too. Dumping them out on the ground, he started to separate them into piles of the same size, and had to pause several times to think they were really his.

"I shall only limit myself to one or two a day." He knew that he'd already used over a dozen of the smaller ones, but that was all right, he told himself. He'd been without for so long, it was a treat. "But no more treats. I must kill Rembrandt, then have his men find me more such stones. I will make a few adherents to help me with this, but I won't be making hundreds. A few very strong good men will get me more than five hundred that cannot think for themselves."

He felt like he'd gained some of his planning skills back as well. He could think out complete thoughts without losing where he'd been. Mary wasn't bothering him now either, not as much anyway. He'd been strong enough to cut her out of his life and to call for Dolin and Ward. They were going to be helpful where Mary had only been mean and hurtful to him. Putting the stones back into the bags now by size, he knew that he was going to win this war against Rembrandt and his brotherhood of fools.

Master wanted to lay out the treasures and look at them again, but didn't. He was fearful that someone would come and see them and try to take them from him. It would be like Rembrandt to do such a thing to him. The man had been most unhelpful in letting him rule, but things were going to change and soon.

"He was never your friend. You know that now, don't you?" He nodded at Dolin when he spoke to him. "If you were smart, and I know that you are, you'd spread the treasures all around your home so that if he should come here he'd not find them all."

"But what if I have a darkness take me? What should I do if I cannot remember where I have stashed them? My memory is getting stronger, but I should hate to lose such a gift. I need to be much better before I do such a thing as that." Ward said that was a good point. That was why he was in charge. "Yes, I am in charge now. You are a good man to finally admit to me being the superior of the three of you."

"I had always thought you to be in charge, Benton. It was Mary that made it so that you were not." Master had always thought that but said nothing. He was going to be kinder in his newfound wealth. "When do you go and get him? I should like to see his face when he realizes that you have bested him yet again."

"It will be a very wonderful day indeed."

Master looked at the bags of stones. Not all of them were ones that had been coveted on the other realm. There were a few diamonds, as well as some red and green stones that he'd mixed with the others. He had wanted to try these out, put them in the chamber of his heart made to hold magic, but he was actually afraid. What if it were to deplete his newly found strength? He looked at his still useless arm and wondered how he would repair it.

"You might be able to cut it off, as you did your tail. It is not any good anyway." He started to point out that he needed it to fly when Ward answered Dolin for him. "Oh yes. But since I do not fly, that might not have occurred to me right away. Yes, I believe him right to have you leave it there. You will need to fly at times."

"Yes, as you said, I can fly so I will just leave it where it is for now. Weak as it is, it still keeps me above the man I wish to kill." And he wanted Rembrandt dead. And that woman of his. "She has caused me much damage in recent weeks. And for what reason, I ask you? I did nothing to her other than try to kill her. That is no reason for her to harm me. If she, like the rest of them, would just do as I have asked, nicely, I might point that out too. But they keep trying and trying to harm me, and now I must make them pay the price."

He pulled one of the bags toward him and dumped the contents on the ground again. They were so lovely, he thought. The colors were brilliant, like someone had polished them just for him. He picked up a green one that had a long white stripe in the middle of it. As he looked closer at it, he plucked two more from the ground at random and put them in his chamber.

"Just in case." He laid the green one down again and made his way out of his dwelling. Taking to the skies, he was amazed at how much power he seemed to have. He could think better too, feeling like he was in control of what was going on in his head. Landing near the building that had given him so much, he went inside again to find if he might have left any behind. It was then that he saw the man.

"You will come with me." The man moved back from him and told him no. "I did not ask should you like to. I said that you will. You will enjoy what I have in mind for you. Serving me will give you the greatest pleasure. You must know this."

When he reached out to grab him, he was thwarted in his efforts when something hit him in the face. As he looked in the direction that it had come from, he saw creatures. Many, many of them. He put out his hand to grab them too. Instead, they parted like the water did when he stepped into it, as if he were nothing more than a pebble to them.

He looked to the man again, to tell him to make them come

to him, and noticed that he was gone. Master peered closer to where he'd been and found a pit in the floor, one with a large door. Tearing it away, he was shocked to see more treasures there, none of them stones like he needed, but things he might use anyway. Everyone knew that if it was hidden away like these things were, they were of value. A value that might come in handy soon when he was master of this realm.

He was looking for more of the nice bags when he heard Dolin tell him he was losing ground again. Master looked to the creatures in the corner.

"Come to me so that I might be able to kill you." The one in front only shook her head. It wasn't until he reached for her that he saw that she had wings. "What are you?"

"Faerie. And we know what you are too. You're a monster." He thought her to be calling him names, but he realized that she might not know any better than to insult him. Her brain would be so small there wasn't any way that she'd be as smart as he was. His brain, he knew, was considerably larger. "What are you doing here?"

"Why, I'm going to rule here. And very soon too. I'm to kill Rembrandt and his men. Then I will use his women to cater to my whims. Dolin and Ward, they came up with that idea and I thought it excellent. When I am—" Ward cut him off. "Oh yes. I'm to focus. Ward is very good at keeping me on track."

She looked around and then at him. "There is no one with you. Are you addled as well?" When she flew closer to him, not enough so that he could touch her but enough that he could see her better, he realized how beautiful she was.

"I'm going to rule all creatures here. I was thinking that I have enough stone dust to perhaps change you into some of the creatures that will serve me. Come closer to me so that I can capture you and try it out. If you die, well, I guess we'll both know that it won't work."

"I'm not going to come to you, you idiot. You're not right in the head." Again he wanted to cut her some slack, a term that while he didn't really understand it, he'd heard Randall say a great deal. "If you seriously think that any of us are going to go to you willingly so that you can kill us, you're nuttier than Lucia is. And she's fucking nuts."

"Such language." He tisked at her and when she laughed, Master felt his temper get the better of him. "Come to me now so that I can kill you. I've decided that I've no use for something so small as you. Rembrandt has made me hurt so I cannot be as quick as I had been. Come here now so that I can end your life and get on with what I was doing before you rudely interrupted me."

"No." He watched her fly around the room and him several times as he tried to swat her. She was like a fly on the ass end of a horse. A fly and a horse. His mind stopped working as he thought of a memory, a long ago one. There had been horses, and he remembered thinking them dirty, so much so that even a fly would not land on them for long.

"Rembrandt wanted me to help him care for his ponies. Ponies, he called them, when everyone knew them to be horses. He was a stupid man. Forever giving things away when he could have bettered himself with them instead. I was always telling him that he should keep his things and not...." He looked at the creature. "Did you know that I murdered his wife and children? I had thought that he'd find it painful when I told him, but he only called me names and shoved me away. Is that any way to treat a friend?"

"Friend? You're not a friend if you murdered his wife and children. And I don't blame him for calling you names.

You should have died instead of them. But I was right, you're a monster." He lunged after her, forgetting that he was still recovering, and his footing got tangled up. When he fell, his big body falling through the floor of the building, he felt a pain near his chamber that had him crying out just before the darkness took him.

~~~

"Is this the last of them?" Rick nodded at Chris and hefted the bag into the back of the truck. To think that had he not walked by the cameras at that moment, they might have had a war on their hands. As it was now, they had no idea how many agates Benton had already taken. Remy was standing in front of the opening of the cave when Rick went back to it.

"What would you do?" He wasn't sure what he wanted to know. Rick would have destroyed it weeks ago when they'd known that Benton was living there. "I know that you were right before, but if we destroy it now, what's to say that he won't find another place, with people this time? Someplace where we don't have cameras?"

"He's been looking into houses. We've seen that. His new weight and size has made it impossible for him to be inside of one for very long." Remy nodded. "If we take care of this place, once and for all, he'll have nowhere to go but out in the open where we can see him. Right?"

"I know not. All I know is that he has done more damage in one short year than most wars have done in decades." Remy sounded defeated. "I'll have Leo and Jamey burn it. At least for a while he won't be able to return here."

When Rick turned back to see what else they could take out of the place, he saw the drawings. Moving deeper into the now emptied cave, he stared at them. Whoever had done them—and he was sure it was Benton—had a violent temper.

And he wanted to kill them all. Taking out his phone, the only thing that he carried anymore that reminded him of the way things had been, he took several pictures and sent them along to the command center. How it worked without Internet service was beyond him, but Rick knew that they'd gotten them when Jake, their go-to guy with the computers, asked for ones that were closer up.

You take the worst pictures I've ever seen. I think young Ruben could do a better job.

He answered his message with a middle finger, another added bonus in being with the Brotherhood that he was sure other phones didn't have, and laughed when he sent him a pile of shit. He was ready to blast back a few more that he'd found when he felt...something.

Hurry to the museum. It wasn't much to go on, but he could hear the urgency in Ryiah's voice. Moving out of the cave, he told Remy and the others to follow him, and those that could took to the skies. Leo stayed behind with Jamey to take care of the cave, while one of the men from the compound drove the vehicle filled with agates back.

Even from the height he was, he could see that Benton had been there. What he didn't understand or couldn't make out was what was crawling all over the outside of the building. When he landed, he realized that it wasn't one thing, but many. The faeries had come to stand behind their mistress. Going to her, he watched as she directed some of the lesser faeries to stand back while the ones with weapons stood guard. Ryiah turned to him when he said her name.

"He tried to kill Hunter and a few of her men. They were scouting around for more of the stones when he came in and told her to come to him." He held her when she seemed ready to collapse. "Hunter was hurt, but she swears that she'll be all right. I don't know what he was looking for. There is nothing in here but a few relics and some displays."

He moved into the broken building with Remy and Davis. When he bent to pick up a flyer that had stuck to his foot, he knew where Benton had gotten his stash of gems and agates. He was ready to turn it over to Remy when he saw that he had one as well.

"It seems that two months ago there was an agate show. They'd been brought in from all over the world so that people could see the different arrays of them. I never thought to come here to check it out." Rick felt sorry for Remy. The man was trying his very best to keep them safe and things kept getting in the way. "Do you suppose he came back here to see if he could find more of them?"

"More than likely. One thing we've learned about Benton is that he's greedy. I mean, most would have been satisfied with what he had, a couple hundred stones to last him a long time. But he had to have more." Remy nodded and asked after the young faerie. "Hunter. Ryiah said that she told her she was fine, but she's sent her to be looked at. Did you know that they have hospitals like we do?"

"I would imagine that their lives aren't that different from ours, wouldn't you?" Rick had a lot to learn about faeries, he guessed. Most of the time, before he'd met and fell in love with Ryiah, he would…. Rick felt himself slide to the floor. "What is it? Are you hurt? Tell me where so that I can have you repaired. Tell me, darn it."

He looked up at his friend. His sword was out and he was covered in the armor that they'd all just learned about. Rick laughed, hard and long, at the picture the man made standing there in shorts and a pair of work boots.

"*Darn it? Darn it?* When a man falls at your feet because

he's only just realized that he's fallen in love with his mate, the best you can come up with is *darn it?*" Remy smacked him in the back of the head. "Well gosh golly gee whiz, Mr. Rembrandt. I didn't mean to upset you any."

"I do not think I care for you anymore." Rick was still laughing when he was helped up by Remy. "But I know what you mean about falling in love and it taking you to your knees. Like you, I thought that I'd had my single chance at happiness. Then along comes a woman that beats everything you've ever had into the dirt, and you're left weak with happiness."

"That's about right." Remy nodded and looked around the nearly destroyed building. Rick did as well. "It looks as if he fell through the floor. I would have thought it strong enough to hold him."

As they looked around, Rick saw a group of the smaller warriors near the other end of the opening and made his way there. Kneeling down so that he was closer to them, he asked what had happened.

"Hunter told us to stand back, so we did." Rick told them that was an excellent idea when dealing with Benton. "When he ordered her to come to him so that he could murder her, I nearly wet myself."

One of the other faeries hit the little one in the back of the head, much as Remy had done to him. He had to hide a smile when they began arguing over the story and how it had played out. When Hunter landed on his bent knee, both of the faeries dropped to the ground and curled their wings to them.

"When he asks you a question, you're to answer. Not argue like a couple of brownies on their first outing." She turned to him. "I am sorry, my lord. I have been working with them. But they're new. I take full responsibility for them being stupid."

"They're not stupid but terrified of me, I think." She looked back at them and then at him again, nodding. "I was trying to get them to tell me what happened. If you don't mind, I'd like to give them practice in talking to me. I know that it's because of what I am."

"Yes, they're not used to a lord that speaks directly to them. Mostly Lord Howard would tell me to talk to them, but I can see where it might be helpful to have them speak to you directly." He nodded. When he'd meant that they might be afraid of him, Rick had meant as a vampire. It never occurred to him that they'd just be afraid of him. He started to ask her who Howard was when she continued. "Lady Ryiah's father was a good leader. He wasn't very abusive, nor did he interact well with what he thought of as his underlings, but he led us into battle well. The mistress, Lady Ryiah, she's told us that we are all together in this or she won't be able to help us. Before we were divided up into groups. A group of us having many battles, and then groups of ones that had less. But she said that we can all have ideas that would serve us well. I think her idea that…she said that we are all to one and one to all."

He corrected her quote. "Yes, Lady Ryiah is correct. We cannot help each other if we're at cross purposes." He looked down at the two faeries. "Please tell me what happened here. And I'd like for you to work together in this story, not tumble all your words out at once as if you don't know what you're doing."

"Yes, my lord." The little blue one said his name was Pitch. The other introduced herself as Whey. Again, Rick had to smile. "We were looking for more of the stones. We knew that he'd taken what was here. Pretty rocks they are. Why he'd want them is beyond —" He looked at Whey when she cleared her throat.

"Hunter was telling us to be on the lookout for him when

the wall just came tumbling down almost on us. We were told to go to the corner and stay, and we did." Rick looked up at Remy when he came to join him just as Pitch was finishing up the rest of his part in the story. Even telling how Benton had climbed out and crawled away. "After he ordered Hunter to come to him, she told him no and then he talked about how he'd been a friend to Rembrandt. And that he'd murdered his family. Like he was proud of that or something. Hunter pointed out that he wasn't much of a friend, and then he came at her and fell."

No one said a word. Rick did look at Remy and saw the man staring off as if he were in pain, and Rick figured that he more than likely was. As he dismissed the young faeries, he stood and turned to Remy. He told him he was sorry.

"'Tis long since passed. I knew that he'd played a part in it…he bragged about it before. But it pains me still. Even after all this time, I see them there. Their faces not so clear, but my love for them has not lessened any." Rick told him again how sorry he was. "They've given us good information?"

"Yes. Benton wanted Hunter to come to him so that he could try and convert her. He must be getting really desperate if he wants to try and convert something so small. Not that she's not scary for her size, but I don't think she alone could harm much." Remy agreed. "Pitch said that when he came out of the hole, he was hurt again. A large piece of some sort of metal had entered his chest. Too bad it didn't hit his black heart."

"Aye, that would have saved us a bit of time had he just impaled himself on a spike." Ryiah asked the faeries if they would look for more of the stones now that they were there, and while there were some, there wasn't nearly the amount that they'd taken from his cave. Rick was sure that had Benton been able to keep them, the war would have started all over again.

CHAPTER 7

Lucia liked the house she was in. There wasn't any magic around and all of her servants were gone, but she'd already decided that when she was finished with this house, she'd simply move to another and then another, until she had to go to another street. But she thought it wouldn't come to that. She'd have Richard where she wanted him and Ryiah would be dead. And once that happened, she'd have her magic back as well.

The faeries had left her, the ungrateful shits. Not a few at a time, but all of them had simply disappeared as if they had an appointment on their calendar. Lucia was going to punish them all as soon as she was in power again. And the first one she was going to take care of was that bossy Hunter. Had she had her way, that bitch would have been dead long ago. For reasons that Lucia did not understand nor like, Ryiah protected that thing with her very life. But after this, she was going to be hers to do with as she pleased, or she'd know the reason why.

Lucia had been planning out her life since she'd figured

out that magic could not just open doors from a distance, but could pull things to her that she wanted without much in the way of effort or expense on her part. She'd had such lovely things as a child, and those things had never gone away when she'd gotten older and her tastes had become much more expensive. So much clothing was in her wardrobe that she'd had to expand her closets so that it would all fit—shoes too. And her handbags had been the envy of every person she ever met. Now it was all gone, thanks to her sister.

Ryiah would have wasted the magic had Lucia not taken it from her. She knew this as well as she did her own name. Where Lucia had made it work for her, Ryiah would let it go, using not just her body to get things done—manual labor, in other words—but she would do it until she dropped. That wasn't what magic was for. But it had gotten her into a few jams over the years.

Several times she'd had to go before the Gathering. And usually she'd have to pay a fine, or worse yet, she'd have to work for them for a time. Of course she never did. Manual labor wasn't what she was meant for. Even when she'd been stripped of her rank and sword by Richard's father, she'd not paid much in the way of comeuppance. The fine, in her opinion, had been paid when they'd made her stop going to the battlefields. But money still found a way into her pocket.

That was when she came up with the idea that Ryiah would get her out of trouble. She would do the things that Lucia was supposed to do, and when finished, talk the one she worked for into giving her a glowing but false recommendation. She supposed it was true for her sister, but Lucia had found the letters sappy and over the top. But even in this, Ryiah had made things difficult for her. Every conversation had ended the same way, with Ryiah making her punish her for something that she'd end up having to do anyway. The first time that she'd told her what to do, Ryiah had told her no. Over and over again.

"You'll go to these events and say you're me. Then I want you to keep it to yourself or I'll take away something that you love." Ryiah had looked over the list and handed it back to her. "You heard me, Ryiah. If you don't do this, I'll take away your freedom and lock you away again."

"What freedom would that be, Lucia? The little that I have when I sleep? You know as well as I that if I don't rest, any of the things you have me do for you, and there are plenty, I'd not have the strength to carry them out in your name. I need rest as much as you." Before she could think of something to take from her, Ryiah continued. "I'm already doing those things on that list from the last time you thought to punish me. My penance, you called it."

"And are you saying that you're me?" She told her no. "Why not? You are to go there and tell them that you lied to them, and then give them my name. I have a meeting with the Gathering soon and I'd like to show them that I have become a good ruler."

"You are not a good ruler. You're a tyrant and mean. You make people suffer for your good fortune. There are times when I think you care not for even me. And I am your blood."

"I don't care for you, Ryiah. I don't think I ever have. As far as I'm concerned, you're nothing but a slave to me, and not a very good one either. I don't care for you any more than I do dung on the bottom of my shoes. But at least with that, I can burn it in the fire. You keep hanging around as if you're wanted."

Ryiah didn't shed a tear that time as she had in the past when Lucia had been particularly cruel to her. And now that she thought on it, her sister had changed after that meeting. It was then that Ryiah started to become mean back to her.

"Well, I won't be having that either. She'll straighten herself up and live by my rules. And if someone has explained to her that she's the eldest, I will have that beaten out of her as well." She'd have to figure out a way to lock her away too, in a dark cell with stone walls and no windows again. The one that she'd used before was in the heap of a house that was no longer fit for her. But she had enjoyed her time away from Ryiah, even though it had made her weak and her magic slower to respond to her commands. "But that certainly made her less sassy after she came out of that place before."

But it hadn't lasted. Ryiah had been getting harder and harder to control of late. Not just refusing to do the things that Lucia had wanted, but she'd also not been as whiny about how she'd treated her. Or how she had others treating her. She'd have to be careful of how she got her sister hurt from now on as well. She had a feeling that Ryiah would report her now, even if she'd not really risen a hand to do anything.

Lucia decided to go shopping and let the bad thoughts work themselves out of her head. Shopping had always made her feel so good about herself. Her mother had liked it as well, but she was gone now, another victim of the Gathering. And, of course, herself too.

After she'd filled the car with some clothing, jewels, and a few other things that she wanted, she tried to find herself a suitable chair, one that she could rule from. There was no doubt that she'd be in charge again. Planning was everything, and Lucia prided herself on being precise on her timelines and getting things done the way she wanted them.

Whatever creatures had come through the town she lived in had certainly made it easy for someone like her to have all

116

that they wanted. She simply had to enter a place, find herself a cart, and take whatever struck her fancy. And a great many things had. She'd filled her cart twice on just handbags alone.

But it was exhausting having to lug everything around that she wanted. For that matter, there were not many people around, fewer than she'd realized, but no one gave her any trouble when she went from shop to shop just taking what she wanted. There wasn't a lot to choose from, but she had made a day of it. It was really too bad that none of the restaurants that were all boarded up had anyone working in them. Lucia went home wondering what she was going to fix herself to eat. Or even how to go about that.

She dragged all her bags into the house and dropped them just inside the door. Next time she'd have to get someone to go with her. This thing with having to do everything on her own was too much work. There had to be someone around here that would want to work for a faerie of good standing. Well, one that appeared to have good standing anyway. She was still grinning about that when she made her way to the living room to rest.

The knock at the front door startled her. Going to it, she had a thought that it might be that creature that she'd seen in town earlier, but realized then that he'd not knock but come right on in. The monster had been talking to himself and speaking in such a slurred way that she'd barely understood more than a few words…Rembrandt being one of them, and bitch the other. For a moment she'd thought him calling her that, but he didn't appear to have even seen her. The second knocking at the door reminded her what she'd been about.

Not opening the door, Lucia tried to use magic to see who it might be. All she managed to do was frustrate herself and give herself a slight headache. Just before opening the door, she heard laughter. She nearly fell back on her ass when she saw what was standing there. The woman looked like...well, a goddess.

"Hello, Lucia. I see that the mighty have fallen this day. But then it's been a long while in coming, so I'm glad to see that it's finally happening." It was in her head that she should be afraid of the creature there, and to bow before her. But instead, she held her ground and had to fight hard with her body not to drop. The creature laughed at her again, and Lucia wanted to hurt her. "You can't hurt me, Lucia, but I might enjoy you trying. And it's only because you have no magic that you can win this war with me. But that won't last either."

"You mean that I shall have my magic back? I never realized how much I depended on it before. Well, I suppose I did, but without it, things are just too exhausting. And I do not care for having to do everything for myself either. I'll take more if you have it on you. If not, you can bring it later. I don't know why it's gone in the first place, but now that you're going to give it back, I'll not bitch too much." The woman didn't even blink at her. "Well? Are you just going to stand there all day or get me my magic? I have to find my...my sister, and bring her to her knees. Then kill my future husband."

Putting her hand over her mouth, Lucia realized how much she'd said. The woman laughed, and this time Lucia thought it sounded like nails on a chalkboard. An expression that she'd never realized how apt it was until now.

"Ryiah, as we both know, is not just your sister but your older sister. And as your elder, you should have been treating her as such. It is a shame that she isn't like you. Not in all things, but in this." Lucia nodded. Her sister wasn't anything at all like her, and she was finally glad that someone was seeing it. "I don't mean to compliment you, Lucia. You're evil and she is not."

"I don't know that I'd go that far in calling me evil, but of course she's not like me. Why is it you think my mother told me to lie all these years? She knew that Ryiah wasn't going to be much use to us. I alone, figured that in order to have the things I wanted the way I wanted, being in charge was going to be what gave it to me." Lucia looked around, then back at the woman. "I just realized that you know all about me, or you think you do. But I don't have any idea who you are. Not that I really care, but should I know you?"

"Yes. All with magic know me. You should have been paying me homage, but like your mother before you, there was nothing forthcoming. You failed in keeping your queen happy." Lucia snorted. "You don't believe that as the queen I should be happy?"

"I think if you were the queen and knowing what you do about me, you'd have killed me by now. Since we both know that you're not going to, I think you should give me the magic you promised me and be on your way." She told her that she'd promised her nothing. "Yes, you did. You said that because I have no magic I can win this war, whatever that might be. Then you said that you'd make that part right. By giving me magic."

"Nay, I did not. I said that you can win against the compulsion I have put against you about bowing, but I never said you'd get magic. What I was referring to was that you won't last much longer." She started to ask her what the hell that was supposed to mean when the woman spoke again. "You will be human when you pass from this world to the next. And I'm sure you'll like it no better than you do lugging around your ill-gotten gains."

"You mean that you're going to kill me?" The woman

shook her head. "Well that's good to know. For a moment there I thought that you had plans to kill me. So back to this misunderstanding about you giving me magic. I don't even know where mine went. I think that Ryiah has gotten it in her head to disobey me and has taken mine. I'd like that returned as well."

"Ryiah was never to obey you at all. And you should know that I shan't kill you, Lucia. Ryiah will." Lucia was shaking her head even as the woman continued. "You have harmed her in ways that should have gotten you killed long ago. Taking her from her element, starving her of the light of the sun. These are only a few of the things that she has against you. There are others, many others that I could name. Like you having her lie for you to the Gathering. That alone can have you beheaded. But that won't happen either. As I said, Ryiah will be the end of you."

"She can't kill me. I'm her blood. I know that. Believe me, I know that. I've been trying to find a loophole in that little bit of magic for a very long time." The woman only smiled at her. "I know what you're thinking. That I've broken the bond. No, I haven't. She's still alive, isn't she? And I've never actually told anyone to hurt her. The man that beat her? I told him to beat everyone he saw. The guy that put her in the dungeon? He told me that he'd thought that Ryiah was going to try and kill me, so he put her there to keep me safe."

"You gave the man who whipped her daily a bonus when you found out that Ryiah was hurt. Of course he would try harder to gain more from you. The man that you claim was keeping you safe? You told him that you thought that Ryiah would harm you in your sleep. And that should that happen, he would be hanged for allowing it to happen. You have set things up so that your lies have double meaning. But I know the truth of it." Lucia said nothing, admitted to nothing either. "Why do you not invite me in, Lucia? I'm sure that we could talk better if you were to allow me entrance."

"I don't think so." Lucia laughed. "If you are indeed the queen, and I'm not saying that you are, inviting you in could mean my death. I don't have any idea where you got it in your head that I was stupid, but I'm not."

"If you think so. So if you won't invite me within your home, perhaps you can come out here on the pretty deck. There are some chairs here that we can rest upon. See them?" Lucia started to go out the door, to step over the threshold, when she realized that was as bad as inviting her in. The woman laughed again, actually threw back her head and did so. "You cannot stay in here forever, Lucia. When you come out, the army that you once ruled with a heavy hand will take you."

"They belong to me." The woman just smiled. "You know as well as I that, as the eldest living child of my father, the horde belongs to me. And that I rule them."

"But you are not the eldest child, are you?" The woman smiled as she continued telling her what she thought she knew. "Have you begun to believe your own lies, Lucia? Are you so mired in your own version of what has happened that you can no longer tell the truth from fiction? You are no more the oldest child of Howard the Warrior than I am his child. And I am much too old to be the child of anyone that ever was. If you wish to believe such things, things that you have muddled in your head, then you do that. But know that eventually things will catch up to you, and it will be Ryiah who is there when it does."

"Go away. I don't want you here anymore. You're... you're messing me up." Lucia looked behind the woman at the faeries there. Christ, there were more than she'd ever seen when she'd helped her father. "What trick is this? How do you make them seem so many?"

"Come out and talk to them, Lucia. I'm sure that they'd be able to give you a first-hand look at how many they really are. Perhaps you can order them to kill Ryiah." Backing from the doorway, Lucia knew that she'd never set foot from this house. Not until she came up with a plan that would bring her sister to her. As soon as she slammed the door shut, cutting off the magic that the woman held her there with, Lucia dropped to the floor. Weakness brought the darkness, and she could no longer fight it.

~~~

Master felt the heat even before he got to the top of the mountain. The trees were scorched and there was no snow, which had been falling since he'd awakened on the ground surrounded by mooing cattle. Moving slowly, not wanting to see what ruin had become his home, he thought of his stones, all his lovely stones.

"I told you not to leave them all in one place." He nodded at the sound of Ward's voice. "Now you have nothing. They cannot stand the heat like other stones can. Even now, if you could get to them, they'd be useless to us."

"I must have left the fire too high when I cleaned my place." He felt the warmth of the hot stones and wanted to curl into it. He sat down, the wound in his chest making him feel lightheaded and weak again. That was when he saw the paper, held down by one of his stones. The pretty green one with a white stripe down the middle of it. Picking it up, almost afraid to see what was there, he saw the drawing of dragons as they sprayed fire at an opening of a mountain. "Ward, what does this mean?"

Master held the note still so that Ward would be able to

see it. There were the two dragons with the fire, but there was a monster too, his head being held down by a great man. A man that looked a great deal like Rembrandt the last time he'd seen him.

"I think he is telling you that he has taken your stones and set fire to your home. See the bags there?" He looked again where the note had been and there they were, neatly folded with a large rock upon them. "Rembrandt also seems to be mimicking your picture, the one on your wall that you drew of him under your feet. You remember that, don't you, Benton? You used several stones to draw it that day."

"No! This cannot be!" Even as he took to the sky, the note still within his hand, he knew that what Ward was telling him was true. Going to the ground below him, landing near the line where he could not cross, he screamed for Rembrandt. Ordered all that were there with a smallish wolf in the yard with them to bring his enemy out to him. While he waited for Rembrandt, he looked at the picture once again.

"You want something, Benton?" Master roared at him that he was Master, not Benton. "You are only Benton to me. Never Master. And I see that you've found my note. It took us a while to figure out how to make you understand, since you've never learned your letters. But I guess you got it. Oh, and we have your agates. It was very good of you to have them ready for us to simply pick up and take. Saved us a great deal of time in gathering them from you."

"You will return those to me posthaste, Rembrandt. Those are not yours to take from me." When Rembrandt crossed his arms over his chest, Master saw stars he was so angry. "You will come to me now and let me kill you. You are nothing to me and I wish you to be dead. I have been very nice to you until now, and I think it is well past time that you are gone

123

from my life. I will wait here for them, but that bitch of yours, she must bring me my stones and I will kill her quickly. You? I think not. I have a need for you to suffer greatly."

"I'm not going to be killed by you, Benton. You have it all fucked up in your head should you think that. When the time comes, and it will be soon, I will take you down and piss upon your feet." Someone leaned to him and whispered. Before Master could demand that he tell him what he said, Rembrandt said he was sorry. This was more like it. "What I meant to say was, I shall piss on your head. Since they look so much alike, I forgot the words."

He felt his darkness spread over him like a blanket. He would almost welcome it to take him, but he feared that if it did, Rembrandt would not play fairly and harm him again. Instead of sliding into it, he fought it by standing up straighter, spreading out his wings behind him. He thought himself impressive until he looked at the creature standing just behind Rembrandt. It moved in a way that made him sick to his belly, to and fro, from side to side like it was a liquid person.

"I would like you to see our army."

He didn't heed what Rembrandt said. Master was too busy watching the thing change with sickening speed. First it was a man, then a monster. A long blade was next, with jewels at the handle and the point. Over and over it moved, changing as quickly as it formed. It was too much, yet he could no more pull his eyes from it as he could remove his broken and injured arm.

"What have you created, Rembrandt? I should like for you to hand it over to me. I will make good use of this sort of magic. It will help me in my quest to kill you." Rembrandt laughed, and Master looked at him. "You will do as I say,

Rembrandt. I think I have been more than generous with you. Especially after all that you have done to me for no reason."

"Generous, you say? How so? When you killed my family? Burned my home down around them? Or when you set fire to my barn, killing defenseless animals while they screamed out their misery?" Master told him that was it exactly. "I see. But there are other things as well, aren't there? Such as when you've attacked innocent people, had monsters take their lives when they did no more to you than I have done. Less actually. I offered you my hand in friendship. You shoved it back at me."

"I've never wished for your friendship. What good would it have done me? How would it have gotten me anything that I wanted? Besides, you would have given it all away had I not taken it from you." He watched the magic and then looked at Rembrandt. "You will do as you're told. I no longer wish to play these games with you. For some reason you have it in your head that you are superior to me, and I will not listen to you anymore. Come now, it is time that you die. And if you bring me my stones, *my stones,* I will not harm the others with you but kill them quickly."

A woman came to stand beside the second man. The look upon her face was hard and unforgiving, and he wondered how he could get her to kill Rembrandt. But before he could come to terms with her, she lifted her arm up and pointed at him. He thought for sure that she was giving him a signal, that she was telling him in some way that he was welcome, when the magic behind her suddenly moved at him.

It occurred to him in that moment what they were. Not magic at all, but bugs. They were the creatures from the building. As he backed from them, their number much larger than it had been at the building, he knew that they were set to hurt him. Why was it that everyone wanted to harm him when he'd done not a thing wrong? But for creatures so small, they were well armed and very practiced at doing it.

The blades in some of their hands cut deeply into the parts of his body where the scales had fallen off. The burning of it had him thinking that there was more to the tiny swords than just metal and leather. Even when he tried to swipe them away from his face and mouth, they moved as one to blind him. One of them, the one that had told him he was stupid, hit him in his eye, and he knew a kind of pain that told him he would never see from that socket again.

Falling back, grabbing anything that he could hold onto, which wasn't much, he hit the dirt. Trees broke under his weight, barely missing stabbing through him. When he looked up, the sky blotted out for a moment as he saw the dragons as they came at him, their beauty nearly making him miss that they were sent to hurt him. Him? They would dare hurt him?

The creatures left him as the dragons came down upon him. Master thought that he was getting help, that Rembrandt had seen reason and was now helping him by having the monsters with flame burn them away. But the fire hit his bad arm and he knew it would never help him now, that flying might not ever be an option for getting away from such meanness. They were hurting him by blowing their heat at every part of his body. As he tried to back away, crawling like a crab would on the sand, his fear doubled when he saw Rembrandt and his bitch coming as well. Turning to his belly, holding his wound at his chest, Master ran. And when he was sure that he could take to the skies, he lifted himself up only to fall back to the earth. Master screamed in pain when he felt Rembrandt drive his blade into his back.

There was no reason for this, his mind screamed at him.

Rembrandt should just let him kill him and this terrible nightmare would finally end. But over and over he was hurt, giving him such pain that he knew should he not get away that they'd surely kill him. And even though he could not fathom why they'd do that to him, Master knew he had to leave, and now.

Running again, trying to get away, all he could think about was that Rembrandt was not playing fairly. That the man was not right in the head to do these things to him. Not just harm him, but to drive a sword through him and end his life. Whatever had he done to have the man hate him so? Nothing. Nothing at all. When he lifted his big body up this time, he was able to get away, flying quick and hard until they were all left behind…or so he had thought, but they followed.

The big body of water seemed to call to him. Diving into it, the pain of it took his breath away, and he inhaled sharply. But the water instead of air filled his mouth and lungs, and he struggled to breath. His head was spinning and he felt weighted down. Grabbing onto rocks as they sped by him, all he could think about was breathing. When pain exploded in his head, he knew that he was dead and closed his eyes.

Richard

CHAPTER 8

They'd been searching for hours. The only thing that they'd been able to find was an arm, and that had been so badly decomposed that no one had wanted to touch it. It had been beaten against the rocks so much that it looked like a mass of raw meat. Putrid meat at that. Rick landed near the shoreline to the fast moving river and stood behind Ryiah, wrapping his arms around her.

"Hunter just heard from the queen of the faeries. She would like to meet with us at midnight." He asked her why midnight. "I asked as well. She told me that it is the bewitching hour. And she also said that there is less going on that needs her attention at that time."

"All right, we can do that. Have you any word on your sister?" She turned in his arms and held onto him as she put her head on his chest. "I'm sorry to have brought it up, love. I only meant to ask so that we could be prepared should she come here."

"Hunter has a few of the people that now work with us watching the house that she is in. I guess she's been shopping too." Rick said nothing. He'd met women like that. A crisis would mean little to them if they could shop it away. "She has no magic. It's been stripped away. Lucia is to stand before the Gathering soon as well."

She nodded. "Have you ever been brought before them?"

"Yes. Many times, but not because of anything that I'd done. Lucia would call me there as her assistant on matters that she'd be in trouble for. She had me pretend to be her so many times over my lifetime that I would sometimes forget who I was. But she had me do it so when asked, she could tell them that she had paperwork showing that she was doing good. My honors and rewards would have her name on them. A faerie must return to the earth and its inhabitants more than they take. I don't know that Lucia ever did her part." He asked if it was a big deal. "Yes, very. They take their jobs very seriously. And her magic, while gone now, the things that she's done could come back to her. The saying that you must give back ten times what you take is true. And if you do not, the penalty for not helping, the magic that you borrow, could take from you ten times ten times ten."

Rick wasn't sure how that worked out, not in terms of magic. He knew that they used a great deal of it here. And he knew that as magical as they all were, they did give back to the earth and land around them, such as planting flowers and trees. Hector told them that for each tree they planted, a great deal of nutrients were put back into the soil. Rick decided that perhaps they needed to do more. He looked at Skylar when she came to them.

"I cannot tell if he died or not. The earth is sort of confused. Even Vicki said that while they can't find the body, they know where parts of him are. Kinda gross if you ask me. Finding that arm will give me nightmares for months." They all laughed.

Rick was pretty sure they'd seen worse shit than most did. "We're going to go back to the compound and hope for the best. Remy and I were wondering if you two could show us a bit more of what is on our bodies. The things you've shown us already have been helpful."

"I can do that." Rick tightened his grip around Ryiah's waist to let her feel his cock. "I have to have a meeting tonight with the queen. I was wondering if you could give me some time first. I need to gather homage for her."

"Great." As Skylar turned to walk away, she smiled as she looked at them again. "Also, I'm guessing that you want to fuck like bunnies in the woods. Sounds like a plan too. I might go and find nice quiet woods for Remy and I while there is little going on."

When she was gone, Ryiah looked up at him with the most shocked look on her face. It was all he could do not to laugh at her, but he was a little afraid of her right now. She also looked like she could do some serious harm to someone.

"She is forever saying things to make me embarrassed. I believe that she does it to.... Well, I have no idea why she does such things. She is...she is a wonderment to me." He kissed her on the nose. "You do that a great deal. I think you think it distracts me from what I'm thinking."

"Or it could be that I want you to think of me and not whatever it is that's going on in your pretty little head." She told him she was forever thinking of him. "And I you. I would never have thought it was possible, but I love you so very much."

"I love you as well. I never thought to have a mate. Never. Lucia worked so hard at keeping me safe. Or her version of being safe. I don't really think it was that she was keeping me safe as much as she was trying to keep me from knowing the truth. I was more like under her thumb. Hunter told me that so long as I didn't have my mate that I'd never come into my own magic. Do you suppose that's why she wanted me dead?" He said he was sure that was it. "I think there is more to this. I mean, what did I ever do to her other than be older? And not by much, only an hour. And you know, had she only asked me, I would have gladly given her all that I had."

"Had you done that she would only have wanted more." He picked her up in his arms. "Now, there was a matter of homage. I would very much like to take you to the woods and pay homage to your body. Tasting it first, then showing you just how good having you wrapped around me feels. What say you?"

"I say that sounds like an amazing idea." As he thought of flying, he took to the skies. He'd not been able to fly before, just move quickly between space and time, but he could see the added advantages of having wings. It was wonderful to be able to see down into areas before taking a mate there to have some fun.

He was kissing her as he landed. Making short work of her clothing and his, he pressed her against the tree that they were near and lifted her up so that she was at his cock. He wasn't ready to take her as yet, but the feeling of her heat touching him so intimately was nearly as good as being inside of her. He set her down on the ground and was startled when she jerked him around so that his back was to the tree and not hers.

"I want to take you into my mouth and feel you coming this way." He nodded, his cock hurting now at the mere thought of her suggestion. "Then when I've had enough of you, which might be a long while, I would like for you to eat me. I think I could come like that all day."

"I have a better idea." She pouted and he laughed. "You can still take me into your mouth, but I'll lay down and you can lay across me." She told him she didn't understand.

Lying on the ground was a little chilly, but the ground warmed almost as soon as he thought of it. When he told her how to lay over him, her pussy at his mouth, her mouth at his cock, she nearly unmanned him in her haste to get into positon. He started to explain what they were going to do, but he nearly came when she took him deep into her mouth and wrapped her hand around what wouldn't fit.

"Christ." This might have been a bad idea, he thought suddenly. She was going to kill him and he'd never get to taste paradise. When she rolled her hips over his face, he suckled her clit into his mouth and was rewarded with a flood of her cream, and cupped her ass to bring her closer. Okay, he thought again, this might be the best way to die, with this woman sucking his cock like a professional and a pussy to feed from.

~~~

His cock was thick with his need, and he was hard in her hand, yet soft at the tip. The different textures of his body, the hardness of his muscles, the buttery feeling of his skin. He was like a walking art exhibit to her. Her very own sculpture that loved her very much.

The tip of his cock fascinated her. The small eye could bring her so much pleasure when it released its hot juices on her. The way that it curved just right inside of her, making parts of her scream for more. Cupping his balls, she realized how hot they were, full as well. Taking one of them into her mouth for just a taste, she was nearly bucked off when he cried out. She smiled, knowing that someday she'd do this again and hope to make him come.

133

Riding his mouth and his talented tongue, all she could think about was how his cock filled her the same way. Much more fully, of course, but his mouth could do so much more. When he suckled her clit into his mouth and bit down, Ryiah came hard and fast, pressing her pussy over his mouth harder so that he'd not stop what he was doing. And when he slid his fingers along the seam of her bottom, her body tensed up, waiting for what things he'd do to her now.

I'd like to take you here sometime. Slide my cock into your tightness. Fuck your pussy with my fingers as you come for me. To have you bent in front of me, your pretty ass tight with need. I'd have to spank you then. Put a print of my hand on your tight ass until you scream out your release. She rode him faster, pressing her pussy faster and faster to his mouth. *Come for me, Ryiah. I want to drink from you this way.*

Her body responded to his command as if he owned her. In a way she supposed that he did. And when she suddenly found herself on her back, she only had a moment to wonder what he was about before he turned her again and brought her ass up to his body. The moment his cock touched her tight hole, she was afraid.

"Don't, baby. It will only hurt for a moment." He slammed forward, the pain of it making her sick to her stomach. When he leaned over her, speaking softly in her ear, she felt her body begin to stretch for him and she listened to him. "I'm sorry. I should have...I shouldn't have hurt you. I'm so terribly sorry."

Moving to take some of the pressure off her knees, Ryiah moaned when his cock moved inside of her. He begged her to stop moving, but her body had other ideas. Lifting her hips up just a little, feeling him shift inside of her, the pleasure outdid the pain of the first invasion and she begged him to finish her.

His hand came down on her ass almost as soon as he sat

up and pulled her hips back. The pain pleasure of the slap made her pussy ache and her ass burn more. The second time his hand came down on her, she did come, a short punch to her system that had her needing more. As he fucked her this way, his cock filling her ass as he never did her pussy, Ryiah slid her fingers down to her clit and pinched it as he'd done.

"Christ, yes. When you come, I can feel it all the way to my fucking feet." He slammed forward again, pushing her head to the dirt more. "Again. Come for me now."

She did, sliding her fingers in and out of her pussy as quickly as he was his cock at her ass. Every time she came, too many to count now, she would feel his hand come down harder and harder. And when he leaned over her, his mouth at her shoulder, she knew that he was ready to come, to fill her, and she was excited. As soon as he sank his teeth into her flesh, Ryiah screamed out her release, the pressure of it just too much to hold inside of her.

When she woke, not even realizing that she'd been out, she was in their room and she was alone. Not that she wasn't used to being alone, but it was somewhat disappointing to wake that way after having such a lovely time in the woods. When the gentle touch of his call to her entered her mind, she stretched out and waited for him to speak to her.

How are you? She told him she would have been better to have had him there. *So greedy. But I'm helping Remy and the others with their marks. I guess because we're bonded I have the same abilities as you in being able to make them out.*

Yes. You will have all that I am. And your abilities, they will be shared with me as well. You're very young compared to me. Were you aware of that? He told her that he'd figured that she was older, but was not positive. *I have been around thousands of years. More than three times as long as Remy. Not as long as Kate — I think she has been around since the beginning of time – but nearly so.*

She's the Keeper of Records. She knew that as well but said nothing. *Okay, the reason that I have disturbed your beauty rest, something you do not need by the way, is that I have found a marking on Remy that I don't understand. I'm not sure if you will either, but it's all wrong.*

I'll come to you now.

Ryiah was dressed when going to the door, and found Hunter and five other faeries there. When she came forward, she could tell that something had gone wrong. Asking her what had happened, Ryiah watched closely when Hunter only shook her head as she flew to her shoulder and landed there. The others came with them, but at a distance this time. "What is it you're not telling me?"

"There is trouble brewing. We can handle it, my lady, but I don't want you to be alarmed." Ryiah asked her to just tell her. "Your sister, my lady. She is causing some issues with the Gathering. She is telling them falsehoods about you."

"I think we talked about this before." Hunter said that they had. "And you know what we must do. I know that you don't agree with me, but it is the only way to keep peace. And there is enough going on without more strife in our ranks. Ask for volunteers to go and help her out. There will be no magic for her, but she will have some help. Perhaps that will calm her a bit and she can think clearly, and maybe she'll tire of this and move on."

"You believe that no more than I do. Lucia will forever want more and take what she does not get. I don't think she will go away without a fight. You know this too." Ryiah said that she did. "I'm sorry, my lady. I know that you are happy, and we are all very glad that you are. But Lucia will need to be dealt with soon. And this will only make her angrier."

"I know. Then I don't know what to do. Tell me, Hunter. Tell me how to make it so that I can go on being happy and have her out of my life." Hunter said that she would think on it, but thought that Lucia needed to be told that she was alone in this war. "All right. But you don't go. I think if she were to have you anywhere near her, she'd try and kill you. And while you're a faerie as I am, you know as well as I do that she can harm you enough that you cannot survive. And that would kill my heart."

"I'll go but will stay away from her. I promise you to only send in the best, and we'll.... I think it would be best if we left her a letter with our intentions on it. That way no one has to be there for any longer than we need be. All right?" Ryiah said that she agreed. "You're a good person, Ryiah, and I love you dearly."

"And I love you more, my heart. Please be careful around my sister. And tell the others to do so as well." They entered the large room where everyone was gathered. "Rick has found a marking that he cannot figure out. Will you see if you know it? If he does not, then I'm not sure I would either."

Hunter went to Remy and asked permission to see the mark. When he turned around, his back facing them, Ryiah saw how much the man had been enhanced since she'd seen him the other day. She stepped forward just as Hunter was studying the lines at his spine. Hunter looked at her when she figured it out as well. It was a mark that she'd not seen in centuries, and even then it had only been a drawing in a book.

"May I see your back, Skylar?"

The young woman turned and took off her shirt. She wore a bra that looked like a very tight shirt, and Ryiah wondered if she could have such a thing. Just as she thought of it, she could feel the difference on her body. It was a nice tight fit, she realized. But she had a task to do before she showed Rick.

The same kind of mark was on Skylar but only half of it, just as it was on Remy.

"My lady?"

It was a mark that could be thought of as very good or terribly bad. Hunter was afraid, but Ryiah knew these two people, and knew that if anyone could be trusted with this magic, it would be them. Nodding to Hunter, she cleared out the other faeries from the room so that they'd not be privy to the magic that Remy and Skylar now held.

"Your mark is the half to a great magic. Skylar holds the other. A magic so powerful and so consuming that it has brought worlds to an end, and created others that have gone on to prosper better than anything ever before it. You both have half of it, as I said, and you must be careful who you tell that you own it." She smiled when Remy and Skylar each took several steps away from each other. "You cannot accidently set it off. There is other magic that must be done to make it work. But you hold something that has been fought and killed over for more years than there has been breath in bodies."

"What can it do?" She looked over at Davis when he asked. "And something this powerful, I'm assuming that it comes with a price as well."

"It does. All magic does. But this particular magic holds the giver in their body long after it is spent. The magic needs the giver, in this case Remy and Skylar, as much as they do the magic they can release. This magic will destroy all that is dead and bring a new life to the land and sky with it." Nate joined them then, and when he was brought up to speed on the conversation, she looked at him. "You hold magic within you too, but I will talk to you about it later. All right?"

"Yes, but I'm sure I don't want to know." She was sure

that he wouldn't. "This magic that they hold, you said it could end the world. That's not what they're to do, is it?"

"No. I don't think that is the reason they have it. I think...." Ryiah looked at Hector. "Your world is gone, you said. Destroyed by the monster that you created?"

"Yes. There is no one left there. The land, too, is dying, as if there is no reason for it to be alive any longer. The few things that I brought here, they are thriving, but not like they did on my planet." She nodded. "You think they are to go there and fix things?"

"I don't know if that is the reason that they have it, but it would fix a great many things. Once the magic is used, the holder, in this case the two of them, would never be able to leave the magic that they created. The land, it would depend on them for all eternity. And once they have children, their children will continue to enrich the land that they created in ways that you've never seen before." Skylar asked her if they were to go to the other realm to do this, what happened to things here. "I don't know. I only know that you carry a mark that hasn't been seen in a very long time, and that the bearer of such a mark would have been chosen by a gathering of people, magical people that would no longer be alive to bear witness to its magic. It would have drained them to have given you such a gift, drained them of every part of themselves. But they would have had to have given it to you freely or it would not have worked. They trust in you; you have no idea how gifted the two of you really are."

"And you cleared out the faeries so that they'd not know. To keep us safe." She nodded and Remy looked at Hunter but spoke to her. "And do you think, with this power, that we were meant to save Hector's world or this one?"

"I know not. As I said, I only know the power of the magic,

not what it is for at this time. I have hopes that this world will be able to come back from this. But I don't know. I'm not sure any of us can know that for sure." He nodded. "Hunter can be trusted, Remy. She would never do anything at all to harm me and mine."

"Why is that? I have a feeling that you are more than just faerie to faerie. I know that she calls you by a title, but I have a feeling that you two are more than that, aren't you?" She looked at Hunter and when she nodded, Ryiah did as well. "And should we know this relationship, one other than just faerie to faerie? For a reason that I cannot put my finger on, I think that it's important that we do. Should you not want to share, then I would understand that as well."

"She created me, as you are aware. But what you don't know is what it took for her to do this." No one spoke as Hunter continued. "When she was locked away long ago, the earth not able to touch her, the sun not there to warm her skin, I was but a small seed, floating upon the small breeze that came through the cracks of her cell. There was no warmth for her, nay, not even a morsel of food to sustain her. But she pulled me to her, cupped me into her hand, and kept me warm. Fed me from her own body by cutting into her skin and putting me there to keep me alive. Dampened my needs with her tears and blood. It also connected us in a way that no other living creature would have had. Her sorrow and heartbreak was what I felt when I grew within her. Had she been different, at a point in her life where she could have, I think her to have wanted to end her life. But she did not. I was there to keep her alive, and she the same for me. Ryiah gave me life because she is the strongest being I've ever met, even stronger than the queen herself, I think."

Hunter bowed before Remy and Skylar before she came

to Ryiah and sat upon her shoulder. Ryiah was afraid they would order her away. That they'd say that what Hunter had said was a falsehood and that she wasn't to be trusted. Rick came forward then and bowed his head to Hunter, and put out his hand for her to come to him. When she did, Ryiah felt her breath hold in her body.

"I'm honored to know you, Hunter. And knowing that you fought so hard to become what you are now, I am in awe of you as well. Thank you for saving Ryiah for us. For me especially." Hunter looked at her before she asked Rick if she could bond with him. "Yes. If you would, I'd very much like to be able to talk to you as Ryiah does."

Her sword didn't look large enough to do much in the way of damage, but Ryiah knew better. It, like her friend, was magical, and small things could hold a great deal of power. When she stabbed the blade into his wrist Rick winced, but he said nothing as she took the blade to her mouth and licked his blood from it. They would never be as close as she and Hunter were, but Rick could summon her as well as the army that she led.

Remy asked if they, too, could bond with the little warrior. They all turned to Ryiah.

"It would be up to her. But know that she does not come alone. There are many that you would command should you need her. It is right that she bond with Rick — he's my mate — but if you take her into your body, her blood with yours, know that she will have an army at her call." Remy asked if they could harm any of them. "She couldn't harm you because of me."

"You'd not allow it." Ryiah looked at Skylar and asked her what she meant. "You would not command them to hurt us, right? I mean, I have a pretty good idea that while they're very small, they can hurt badly. And it would be nowhere close to what they did to Benton the other day."

"I cannot." They still looked confused. "We are family. The same as if we had shared the same parents. It's what makes you so strong. The way you can depend on each other to have your backs. Trust is there, as is love. Friendship that is stronger than any ties known to humans. We cannot harm each other because we are family."

Everyone looked at Remy. "If one of you says that I am the daddy in this mess, I shall test the theory that I cannot hurt you. To the very limits of it." They laughed and Ryiah watched them. To have had family like this growing up, she might have been a lot better person today. Skylar turned to her then.

"You are a wonderful person, Ryiah. A good friend to us all, and I for one am glad to call you sister." Ryiah felt humbled at such a compliment, and nodded. "Now, if you can figure out a few more of these marks on us, I for one will be thrilled to death. Oh, do you know if there is anything here that says that I'm smarter than Remy?"

"You are, love. And you always will be." Remy hugged his mate to him as he continued. "And the both of us are much smarter than any of these fools."

After that, it was a free for all in making fun of each other. The kidding continued long after she gave them more information, and even at dinner, where they all met when they could nightly. Ryiah had never been this happy before.

Richard

CHAPTER 9

Lucia wasn't happy. She was bored to death, and she had run out of things to do several hours ago. Ignoring the constant knocks at her door, she was tempted to open it just to have someone to talk to. But to do that could invite in trouble that she just didn't want to deal with.

Going to the bedroom that she'd moved into just that morning, she looked around at what was obviously a little girl's room. If there had been any other room she could have used, she would never have stepped in this room willingly. It was just too…pink. Walls, rugs, covers, even the sheets were pink. And a color so ugly that she thought someone had made the color up. There was no way that it came from something of this earth. But it was either move in here or take the chance to leave the house and find another one. And that seemed too dangerous at the moment.

The three bedrooms that she'd used up until now were messy. And since there was no one to come and clean up after her, not even to make the bed, she wasn't going to be staying where it wasn't fit. If only she could find one person that she could trust to do things for her.

Grabbing the bag of potato chips, a treat she'd never had until the other day, she ate them while walking around the room. Not only was everything pink, but there had to be five hundred dolls and stuffed animals.

"Why? Why would anyone need this many...what is this thing? Tigers. Who needs ten different-sized tigers in one room?" She tossed the animal behind her as chips fell from her fingers. "And this? Why does she have so many books? There is no reason to fill a room with books when there are so many other lovely things to have in a room. Like clothing and shoes."

By the time she was standing in the bathroom, Lucia had decided that the child was colorblind. There wasn't any way a person could put zebra stripes on the wall and have a pink counter and rugs, as well as a shower curtain to match, and not be physically ill all the time. Ripping the offending curtain down, she decided that she'd bathe from now on in this room and not shower. This just wasn't what she wanted in a house.

"The next time I go house hunting I'm going to go through the entire thing before I pick. Just because it is glamourous on the outside and around the front entrance does not mean that it has anything worth looking at inside." Lucia heard the knocking again and screamed. "Go the fuck away."

When the knocking continued, as if there were more than one person at the door and they were taking turns, Lucia stomped down the stairs to tear the person there a new ass. If she'd had any magic, she would have blasted them out of this realm and into the next. This was bordering on harassment. As soon as she opened the door, she knew that she'd made a huge mistake. Again.

"Lucia Alvarez, you are hereby summoned to the

Gathering."

And just like that, she was standing in the large open area again. This time they'd not just clasped her hands together in front of her, but had shackled her ankles as well. She tried her best to look as innocent as she could. No one said a word to her, but they did talk between themselves. When it was obvious that they weren't going to tell her why she was there, she cleared her throat. They all looked at her as if they had no idea she was there.

"I'd very much like to be returned to my home. And if you could see fit to return my magic, that would be great as well. I did talk with a woman in white and she said she'd return it to me, but so far I've seen nothing. I've been having some issues at home, and I can only imagine why you'd think to take it from me." They stared at her. "Hello? I'm asking for your help. Can you just send me home? Please?"

"You've been brought here because of the issues that you're having at home. We have received all of your complaints about your sister, as well as a faerie that you call Fucking Hunter. Which, I must confess, we cannot find on our rosters." She wanted to go over there and bash his head in. She'd just said that she was having trouble at home, and the fact that they couldn't find Hunter wasn't her concern. Lucia just wanted her dealt with and out of her life. "And we did not take your magic, Lucia. It was given to the rightful owner of it. Now, you have been found guilty of the charges of—"

"Hold on there a minute. I know my rights. I'm to get a hearing and then you debate. You might have debated on the information that you think you know, but it's not the truth. Not any of it." He asked her how she'd know that. "Well, I don't know, but I'm pretty sure that you don't bring a person here and slap chains on them if you think that they're not guilty. I've done nothing wrong. And I can prove it if you just bring the thief here and let her explain why she's taken what doesn't belong to her."

"What of your lies about your sister, Ryiah? You have kept her in the dark concerning her birthright, as well as used her as a slave for many centuries. That alone is enough to get you fined, as well as some time in the cell." Lucia smiled. She had this one answered. "If you think there is anyone that would come to your defense on this, please call them out. I should like to know the reasons for you acting so against one of your blood."

"My sister, Ryiah. She is a little off in the head. That's the reason that I've been taking care of her. And what do you think might have happened to the magic had she had any of it? I can tell you, it would have been bad. Especially for me and my family. But if you'd allow me to return to my home, I could show you the documents that she signed giving me permission to take the magic that was allotted to her by our father." He asked her what she meant by "off in the head." "You know. Her brain doesn't work like everyone else's. I've been sheltering her all her life, you see, but I think you need to understand what I've been having to deal with. I've not let on how mean she can be nor how she lies about everything. Like me trying to have her killed or even taking things from her that she claims belong to her. Then I'd like to have my magic returned, that I'm assuming you gave her when you took it from me. I have the paperwork right at home."

"No, I don't think it will do any of us any good should you leave here without this being resolved. I suggest that we bring her here to speak before us." That wasn't going to work for her, so she told him that she was in a home under constant care. "Be that as it may, I, for one, would like to talk to her."

"You see, that's what everyone says. Then when she starts going on about things that never happened, it's hard on people. She might be on this kick where she talks about having a mate. Or that she commands armies. You know as well as I that I'm the one that did that. I think she's been jealous of me all these years and it has gotten mixed up in her head somehow. Like I said, she's off in her head all the time."

When they conferred again, Lucia looked around. That was when she saw that little faerie that had been bothering her for days now. Hunter. She'd only answered to Ryiah for some reason even before Lucia's magic was stolen from her. So when Hunter waved and blew her kisses, Lucia knew that she was going to find her when this crap was finished and end her life.

"We have decided to suspend things for the time being."

Lucia let out a long breath and thought of all the things she was going to do as soon as she was free. First and foremost, she was going to find a place to hide. Somewhere that she could get servants to work for her in. She asked them about her magic. After another long talk, the woman closest to her smiled.

"As we have stated, we don't have any magic that belongs to you. Your sister has it, and will keep it until such time that we can listen to her side of the story." Lucia offered again to go and get the paperwork. "That won't be necessary."

"Good. But then how do we go about getting my magic back from my sister? I really could use it, and I've been without it for a very long time."

They spoke together once again. She wondered if one of them had to use the bathroom, how long it would take before someone pissed themselves before they made a decision. Hunter flew to the table and joined in on the talk. This was going to take for-fucking-ever.

"We will speak with your sister. And when we have come to a decision, we will bring you forth. Until such time you will live as you have been, without magic." At a nod to Hunter, the little faerie came to her. "Hunter and her men will see you to your cell."

"Cell? No. I don't want to be in a cell. You said I could live as I was before. I can do that, but putting me in a cell just isn't right." Even as she was taken away, her body no longer obeying her but that of the faerie that led her, Lucia was still screaming at them to let her go back to her home. "This isn't right. I'm the oldest. You must let me go. I demand it."

As soon as the magic closed around her, she knew that she was as good as dead. Hunter flying in front of her did nothing for her temper. But instead of unleashing it on her as she wanted, she took a deep breath and thought of all the things this little bug could do for her.

"I would like for you to take my sister a message." Hunter said nothing but watched her. "Tell her that I'm in trouble and I'd like for her to come here and talk to me. Tell her that if she doesn't, I could die."

"And how do you think that is going to make her want to come to you? You should have been beheaded decades ago, Lucia. You've been nothing but trouble since your first breath." She wanted to reach between the magic and kill the little fucker, and the only way that Hunter could ever be killed was if she had her neck broken or her head removed, and that wasn't going to happen soon enough for Lucia. Breaching the magic between them was impossible. "I might take her a message for you. But I won't make her unhappy. She's in a wonderful place right now, and I don't want to upset her."

"She should fucking be here instead of me." Lucia closed

her eyes before continuing again. "I need her to come here so that I can tell her what to say to the Gathering. If she doesn't, I won't be there for her anymore."

"You've never been there for her. Again, you're going to have to do much better than that. What is it you think you're going to get out of me telling her that you wish for her to lie for you? That is what you want, isn't it? For Ryiah to lie to the Gathering? You do know that they'll kill her if she does." Lucia wanted to tell her that she didn't care what happened to her sister so long as she was free, but knew that would be the wrong thing to say as well. "I have things to do, Lucia. Come up with something better or I'm leaving you here to rot."

"I hate you. You know that when I'm free I'm going to make it my business to figure out a way to have you murdered, even should I have to do it myself. Why you're so important to her is beyond me, but I'll fix your ass." Hunter just laughed. "Tell her to come here today. That I need to speak to her before she comes before the Gathering."

"Won't be today, I'm afraid. She's got an appointment with the queen." Lucia asked who that might be. "The queen of faeries. You met her the other day. She went by your home and warned you off coming out. Just so you know, we couldn't have done a thing to you should you have left your house. We can only attack by one person's command, and I don't think Ryiah cares if you live or die."

Lucia was still thinking how she'd been tricked when her meal was delivered to her. There wasn't a person that she could talk to; magic set it on the small table that was there. And Lucia knew that as soon as she was finished eating, if she ate any of it, the tray and the table would disappear. She was going to be taken care of, but there was no one to complain to should she want to. She was cut off from everyone and everything. Lucia hated them all.

~~~

Remy looked at the pictures that had been taken of his body and stared at the one of his spine. He could see it now; when he laid the picture of Skylar next to it, he could see where they fit together. Not only that, but they seemed to jump right out at him when he stared at them long enough. When someone sat down across from him, he stared at Hector.

"I wish to request that you do not waste the power that you have on my realm." Remy said nothing, not even sure what he would say. "I have given it a great deal of thought, and after talking to Ryiah a little more, I think that you going there would be a mistake. And even though I miss things there, this is my home now and there is nothing left there."

"Ryiah said that once the magic is unleashed, everything there would disappear and it would be like a clean slate. Nothing, save the Keeper, would be left of it. Then the magic in us would take over and all forms of life, in the way of the earth, would start to grow. Later, when there was enough food to support it, other creatures would arrive, as if drawn to the place." Hector nodded. "Tell me really why you don't want me to do this. I know that this is yours and Ruben's home. And I'm not saying that we will, but we both know that's not the real reason."

"You will be there and not here." Skylar and he had talked of that as well with Ryiah. She explained that should they leave for a few days, even a week, things would go on. But anything over that and the world would die. And in turn, so would they. The connection between them and whatever realm they created would be as tight as a seed to the plant that grew from it. "I would miss you both. I know that the rest of us would as well."

"And you don't think we'd miss you as well?" Hector nodded. "There is no reason that you cannot come to visit us, Hector. If we were to do this, we'd love to have all of you come and stay with us. It would be a world like none other."

"I had thought that before. I thought I lived in a utopia. But my wife, she died there. Along with a great many of my friends. I'm not sure I'd be able to go back and not think of those things." Remy told him he was sorry. "As am I. I think of all the things that we have brought here to your planet. The destruction of your world and the people that lived here. So many deaths. And for no other reason than greed."

"Hector, it wasn't your fault. None of this was. And you changing me when you did.... Well, had you not, I would not have met Skylar and the rest of the Brotherhood. I cannot thank you enough for that."

"At one time you wished for me to die and to leave you in peace." Remy nodded and smiled. "You saved my life more than I changed anything in yours. Had you not taken my son that day and worked so hard for all of us, there would be no Ruben nor myself. This world, too, would be nearly as destroyed as my own is. You are a great man, Rembrandt. In that, I have to say I was right."

"You are a good man as well, Hector. But we are getting upset over something that we don't know will happen. Skylar and I, we have spoken with Ryiah as well. She is...I think once she has more confidence in herself, she will be able to take on Benton all on her own. She's scary like Skylar and the rest of them are. And I don't want to think of things like new worlds until we have this one in better shape than it is at the moment." Hector agreed with him. "Hector, do you think him dead? Benton...do you think when he fell into the water, that he was killed?"

151

"Do you?" Remy shook his head. "I do not either. I think that he will need to die at your hands, all of yours. And while he might be down and in, I think that's correct, he will not go down so easily."

"Down and out. But I think you're right." He glanced at the pictures again. "Ryiah said that this was fae. A long ago language and magic that even the fae of now do not use. That our bodies are marked with hundreds of dialects, as well as other magical languages, that we might not ever learn where they came from."

"I've been thinking on that as well, and I have a theory. What if the earth, which you are a large part of, decided to band together and help you? The fae and faeries, as well as the earth and other elements. There are hundreds of creatures that live here that we might not even realize. What if they all put this magic on you with the thoughts of making you the strongest person in both magic and strength to save them as well?" Hector got up to pace, something that most of them did when they were working on something, but Hector seemed to have a passion for it. "I changed you that way only in that I made you immortal as well as healed you. Strength you had. Plenty of muscle as well as fortitude. But that day, you spilled your blood on the earth. I think in that, even it knew that you were the man to save it as well as make it better."

Remy thought on that. It made sense. Not that he thought himself any different than many other men out there on that field, but he had been the one that Hector had chosen. He'd told them from the start that he'd only saved them to do the job, and had not marked them as they were. Perhaps this was just the way he'd said, the earth as well as other magic had decided to help them.

"Do you still think that when the last mate comes here that

she'll bring us such magic that we'll be able to conquer this?" Since, like him, they didn't believe that Benton was dead yet, he needed to know that they could fix things here. "I'm not sure if I want to think about what she'd bring to us. I think us pretty powerful as it is."

"But you see, I don't think she'll bring magic that will kill Benton. I think she will be a part of the whole of you. Her magic, whatever it might be, will be the key to bringing him down, but only because of the rest of you. A link in the chain, I think." Remy asked him why he thought that. "Because, my good friend, it's what I need to believe. As a whole we've done much. The malefactors are not as many. Dolin and Ward are gone, and we're not working nearly as hard as we were in trying to figure this out. With the help of each person that comes here, we've learned a great deal. People are talking to each other, getting along, and sometimes when necessary, when they need to work things out, they do, not with fists or guns but with words."

"Aye. And we've new life too. Not just from the people coming here, but new babes as well. Just yesterday we had two being born. That's what I wish, for us to be a human race again." Hector said that he thought they would be. And soon. "Yes, I think you're right. I believe it too."

Standing up, he stretched. Hector, even with them being as good of friends as they were, still backed from him when they were together. Remy had thought at first he was afraid of him, but Skylar pointed out that with his size, Hector was fearful of being in the way. It was not that he was being rude or afraid, he wished only to give Remy space.

"I think that we should have a party. A large one too. With food and friends aplenty." Hector laughed and agreed with him. "I'll leave talking to Ann about such an undertaking to you. The good woman would do just about anything for you."

"No. Oh no. We're just good friends." Remy watched his friend as he seemed to think things over. "You don't think she's falling in love with me, do you? I shouldn't know what to do with.... How does one...? Remy, I think I shall have to think on this."

Remy was still laughing when Hector left him. He had no doubt that the man would have graphs and charts trying to figure out this deepening friendship between him and Ann. Remy would admit that he'd not seen it, but Skylar had. She told him that it would be good for the two of them, as they had a great deal in common. Not to mention, she thought them in need of each other's company. Remy wasn't so sure, but if they were happy, then he was.

As he made his way into the yard, he thought of the things that he and Hector had discussed. Bending to his knee, he put his hand on the earth and felt it warm beneath his hand. Thinking again of all the harm that had been put upon it, he thanked it for its nourishment as well as its help.

He felt the movement before the grass seemed to reach up and wrap around his fingers. It wasn't painful, not in the least bit, but Remy was a little nervous. Trying to think what to say to grass and the soil beneath it, he felt...well, Remy felt refreshed. Stronger and rested.

"Thank you, my lady." The grass tightened around his fingers for a second, then loosened again. "I have taken much advantage of you, I think. We all have. And after all you've done for us."

When the soil came up and touched his fingertips, Remy dug them deep into it. When he felt the connection, he sat down. Christ, all he wanted to do was be a nicer person to the earth that had fed him over his lifetime.

You are a good man, Rembrandt the Warrior. He said he was but a man, and didn't feel the least bit afraid that he was hearing the ground speak with him. *Nay, you are more than that. You are everything that we had hoped for when this war began. More if you wish the truth of it. We have provided for you as much as we could. The earth yet owes you more than you can know.*

"I should like to repay you for our food and warmth. The way that I've only just realized that you made us safe with your magic. Provided for us in ways that we never thought of." She told him it was her pleasure. "I'd like to do more for you, my lady. Tell me what it is and I shall do my very best to give it to you."

I should like plants. Trees as well. Fruit-bearing ones so that their seeds can propagate and grow more. Flowers and bushes. Flowering plants for the bees and faeries. I'd like for you to, if you could, make us fruitful again. Give us a reason to live. He told her he'd do that and more. *Thank you, Rembrandt the Great. Should you need me, or any of my sisters as well, you need only to call out to us. Touch us as you are now and we can give you what we can.*

Standing up after telling her again that he'd help, he looked around. Yes, these were things he could do. Things that he'd done in his life before becoming a warrior for Hector. Going to find someone to go with him into town to look for seeds and saplings if he could find them, his mind was working on plans to get them into the ground. He decided that he'd make this a daily project for himself. And if the others would like to join him, he'd welcome them.

CHAPTER 10

Ryiah moved to the cell where her sister was. She'd made such a nuisance of herself that the Gathering had asked her to come see her. She explained to them that she wasn't ready to see her just yet, but they said that it would go a long way to getting answers should she do them this favor. She told them she would, but she'd have to have someone with her.

The Gathering had been around since before she'd been born. Most of the time they would only be asked to preside over something when it involved not just murder, but a disregard for everything that magic stood for. The seven men and women brought with them years of experience, as well as a vastly different kind of information about any particular paranormal. They were, as their name implied, a part of the whole of all magic there was.

As soon as she saw her sister, Ryiah knew things would not go as well as the Gathering had hoped. But they'd asked her to see if she could come to some arrangement to set her free. A freedom, they assured her, which would be short-lived. But they needed more evidence against Lucia to make their ruling more complete.

Lucia was the same as she'd been when they were children, expecting things to be her way, and damn those that wouldn't see it that way. Whatever they had planned for her sister, she'd make sure they did it. Ryiah would be glad to have her out of her life. Prison in the dungeon was just what she deserved.

"Lucia." She stood up and came to the magic that held her there. When she asked her about Rick, she told her. "This is Rick. You might have known him as Richard James. We're mates."

"No. That can't be. I didn't give you any leave to take a mate. No, that won't be happening. As soon as you get me out of here, we'll have to figure out how to make this right. You cannot have found a mate in the man that I was to have as mine." Lucia looked at Rick then. "You certainly are more than I thought you'd be. Why did you let yourself be all marked up that way? Well, for that matter, the two of you. Whatever magic you used on each other will be returned to me as well. I've been punished long enough for your misdeeds."

"*My* misdeeds? What on earth can you have in your sick mind that you think I did to you?" When Lucia started to speak, Ryiah cut her off. "You know what, I don't really care. Whatever comes out of your mouth right now, I'd not believe you anyway. I'm sure you think you have some sort of justification for how you treated me."

"I did nothing to you that you didn't deserve. And as your sister, your only living relative, I demand that you get me out of here so that I can take back what is rightfully mine." Ryiah asked her what she thought that might be. "Well, first and foremost, my magic. You're going to return every bit of it to me. Also, this sham of a bonding. That will have to be taken care of as well. With you having a mate, the magic is stronger. I'll have to either kill him or you give him up."

"No." Lucia just laughed. "I'm not going to get you out of here, not without conditions. I'm not going to give up Rick, nor am I going to turn any magic over to—"

"What sort of conditions?" Ryiah glanced at Rick when Lucia continued. "Still can't make a fucking decision on your own, can you, Ryiah? No matter. I was always better at it anyway. So what conditions do you think to impose on me to get me out of here? I'll do it. I just need to get out so that I can get my shit together."

"You'll not come near me or mine." Lucia nodded and Ryiah didn't believe her. "You'll live your life as a human. Giving back to the earth all the magic that you took from it and never returned."

"Why should I do anything like...? Never mind. Yes, I'll do that as well. What else do you want? My money? You took that when you left me there to fend for myself. How about my magic? You stole that from me as well. Just went out and did what I tried to keep you from doing all your fucking life. A mate, Ryiah? You found a mate when I wanted you dead? How could you?"

"I could do it because I got away from you. Started to realize that you're not at all a nice person. Not that I didn't already know that, but without you in my life I've enjoyed myself. Had fun. Laughed with new friends." Lucia started mocking her, flapping her fingers to her thumb in a way that hurt Ryiah. "You'll abide by these rules or you'll find yourself back here and in the worst kind of cell."

"When? When are they going to free me?" The paper appeared in front of her and Lucia snatched it up without reading it. When magic presented it before her, Ryiah signed it as well. Anything to get this over with. When the magic was dropped at the door, Lucia walked by her without a word. Ryiah looked at Rick.

"It won't last, you know that, right?" Ryiah nodded and moved to get comfort from Rick. "I look for her to be arrested again by the end of the day. And when she is, we'll not come back here no matter what they say. This has been hard on you."

"I'd like to go home, please." He nodded but held her in his arms. "I haven't had any feelings for her for a very long time. I can't even remember the last time that I thought of her as a sister and not some monster."

"She made it difficult for anyone to like her. And the fact that she sees nothing wrong with what she's done shows just what sort of person she really is."

They started for the door and were stopped by Hunter.

"My lady, she's trying to rule us. I should like your permission to ignore her when she calls to us." Ryiah asked her how she was able to do that without magic. "She has our blood. It was given to her when we were on the battlefields. Not all of us, mind you, but enough for us to be afraid when she does it. Her connection to us could be our downfall."

"You have my permission to do whatever is necessary to keep all of you safe. When she summons any of you, you will go to her at your own risk." Hunter smiled, then bowed before leaving. "I'm assuming that she wanted the army at her beck and call to end my life. I don't know how she would be able to do it; I'm assuming because she thinks that I've grievously harmed her. That is all it would take to let her use them against me."

"You can do the same, can't you? Call them against her should you need to?" She told him that they both could.

"Then we'll keep an eye on her so that when she fucks up, not if but when, we can take care that we end the world of her darkness."

"Rick, take me home and make love to me." He lifted her in his arms and Ryiah felt safe and secure. "What would I have done had you not wanted me? Or I'd not come to the compound to find you?"

"Neither of our lives would have been complete." She found herself in the bedroom and naked. When he stood over her, his body as hard as hers, she reached for him and he came to her gently. Softly. "I love you so very much, Ryiah. More than I could ever put into words."

"Then show me." He touched his mouth to her breast, then the other. As he kissed her body, he touched her as well. Every part of her yearned for him, yet she felt that waiting for him to take her was going to be what they both needed.

~~~

Rick wanted to savor every part of her body. Not just the flesh that was hers but her soul, heart, and mind. She was his, in every sense of the word, and in turn, he belonged to her as well.

Taking her nipple into his mouth, he suckled just the hard tip. He knew that she loved this, her body bowing up for him to take more of her. But he wanted to go slowly. Have her pleasure come to her over and over until he took his own. When she curled her fingers into his hair and held her to him, he looked at her while he bit down hard enough to draw blood.

"Yes," she cried out as her body shuddered beneath his. He suckled harder, drinking deeply from her before moving to the other breast to do the same. As she held him to her, he moved his hand down her body, cupped her ass, and brought her closer still to him.

She was hot, wet, and he wanted to take her then. But he also wanted her to forget about the day they'd had so far, the treatment from her sister. Moving down her body to her navel, he licked the tiny indention before moving back up to her throat and earlobe. Ryiah cried out again, but she was rolling her hips in such a way that he knew he could easily slide into her.

"Please? I need to feel you." Rick teased her with his cock, his crown barely breaching her as he fucked her slowly. "You're killing me. I want to feel you fucking me."

"You will." He moved over her again, sliding in and out of her as sweat slid down his spine. "Do you have any idea how much I love you?"

She nodded and he pulled free of her. "Yes. I know. Yes, please. I hurt, I need you so badly. Please?"

"The thought of plowing you, taking your pussy over and over while you hold onto me. Feeling your sheath strangle my cock with your release. I love the way your nipples harden; the way your breasts seem to swell just before you come." Her soft growl had him laughing. "Come for me, Ryiah, and I'll show you with my body how much I love you."

Her scream seemed to come from her feet. It was loud, long, and gave him the perfect opportunity to fill her. When she came a second time, then a third and fourth, he knew that if he didn't come soon, he'd be in a great deal of pain. But before he could finish them both, she rolled him to his back and sat over him. All thoughts of rushing to the end evaporated in that minute.

With her hand on his chest, she rode him hard. Her hips rolled over him much like a cowboy did a bull. Smiling at the thought, he rolled his own hips upward and watched her face when she came again.

"I love how deeply you fill me." Rick grabbed her hips and held on. He didn't want to stop her, nor to slow her, but he felt like if he didn't keep holding her that one or both of them would fly away when their climax took them. "I need to take you."

Rick tilted his head to give her what she needed, but when she ran her fingers over his chest, where his heart was, he pulled her wrist to his mouth and waited. The moment that she came, he was going to bite her and fall over the cavern with her.

Her mouth moved over the wound at his chest. When she drew deeply, he licked the pounding pulse that he held in his hand, and when she came, he pulled her closer to him with his free hand and bit down into her wrist at the same time.

The explosion in his body seemed to take forever to peak. But once it did, it took not just his breath away but seemed to stop his heart as well. Then he cried out around her flesh when she dug her own nails into his ass. Rick came three times, sharp hard punches to his system. He next rolled her to her back and took her again. Christ, he'd never get enough of this woman, he thought.

He brought her to climax three more times, and held her when she went limp. He knew that she'd passed out. And while he was very proud of his performance in that moment, he was also very happy that she wasn't shy about hard sex. Christ, the woman was going to kill him.

Rolling to his back, covering her as he did, Rick sat up on the side of the bed and dressed. He watched her rest, knowing that when she woke again she'd be just as stressed as she'd been before her visit with Lucia. Ryiah hadn't been sleeping well and he was concerned that she was going to be hurt by Lucia. More so than she had previously.

I was wondering if you could come and help me with something. Rick stood up and moved to the door as Nate continued to speak to him from the link that they all had. *I have some information that you might want to pass on to Ryiah. Or not. I don't know what I'd do if I was mated to someone that is.... Can you come to the command center?*

I'm on my way. And if this is about Lucia and her being free, we know that. Nate said that he figured they did. *And the faeries aren't to go near her.* Hunter said that they were connected by blood.

Yeah, that explains a lot. Rick asked him what he meant. *You should come here and let me show you. That freaky thing I can do with computers? Well, apparently I can do the same with cameras. More than likely any kind of connected service like that.*

As soon as he entered the command center, Rick wanted to turn back and go to Ryiah. He had a feeling that whatever was going on, she was going to be involved. Nate showed him what he'd found.

The room looked normal enough, messy and like someone had had a fight in it, but he wasn't sure what else he was to be looking for. When Nate zoomed the camera in on a small part of the room, it took Rick a few seconds to figure out what he was seeing.

"That's Hunter." The little faerie wasn't moving, and it looked as if someone had put a glass or something similar over her. "She'll die if she hasn't already."

"I don't think she's dead. I don't know why that is, but I don't think that she is. But what I can tell you is that she's been lying that way for several minutes. At least since I called to you. I have a feeling you know where she might be." Rick nodded but never took his eyes off the little warrior. "I'd say she went there to tell Lucia that they were finished and she somehow ambushed her. I don't know a great deal about

164

the magic that the little one holds, but I'd say that Lucia was waiting for her."

"What is that over there?" The camera moved in to where Rick pointed. "Christ. I'd say she was waiting. Is that a badminton racket? You don't think she hit her with that, do you?"

"I'd say that's a good possibility." Both Nate and he looked at the door when Ryiah spoke. "She's hurt badly and cannot move, and her air has been cut off too…I'm assuming by the glass that is over her. I have to go there and get her. There are others there with her, but they cannot go to her. Lucia has them all terrified. Can you go back, look at the room?"

As they did that, the camera panned around and they saw her there. Lucia was standing on a table and swinging at anyone who got close enough for her to hit. Two other faeries lay on the floor, and one of them looked broken. Rick asked her what she wanted to do.

"End her." Rick was all for that, but they needed a plan. Ryiah said she was working on that and had called the queen. He had a feeling that she'd not meant via the phone either. And when the woman appeared in the room, Remy and Skylar came in through the doorway.

"I should never have canceled that appointment that I had with you several days ago. Perhaps had I not been too busy, I might have been able to tell you that Hunter was in trouble." The queen looked visibly upset. "I cannot beg your forgiveness enough for this. We must go and get her at all costs. Hunter is very special to me as well. All of my faeries are."

Rick had forgotten about that. They were to meet her at midnight and talk. But at the last minute the queen had sent a message telling them that something had come up and that they'd have to do it another time, but soon. Ryiah asked what they could do about Lucia now.

"As you have said, she must die for this. Two of the others, the smaller faerie, have died. And several more have been injured when they went to help Hunter and the others." Rick looked at Ryiah, knowing that she was worried about Hunter. "I've sent someone in to get them. They should be —"

"No. I have this." Rick wanted to protest, tell Ryiah that was a terrible idea, but she continued. "She's doing this because of me. Not that it justifies it, but she's hurt Hunter because she knows how much she means to me. And the others because she's lost something very precious to her. Fame and magic."

"You might have to kill her, Ryiah. I can do this for you. It would be my pleasure. When she harmed one of mine, she ended all good will I have toward her." Ryiah shook her head, and before he could try again to say something, Skylar spoke to him through the link that they'd established recently.

If she doesn't do this her way, it will haunt her. She already feels guilty that she had her released and the Gathering didn't do as they said and keep her under control. Rick said that it was her sister. I think that relationship ended a very long time ago. You should ask Ryiah sometime about some of the things Lucia had her do. Or did to her. They were never a family. Not even when they were children. If I were you, I'd support her and help her. She's going to need you.

After thanking Skylar, he leaned back and decided that he would only voice his opinion on this if anyone asked. And he also thought that Skylar was right. He had felt the guilt eating at her even as Lucia left them in the cell area. Ryiah would have known then it was going to end this way. But he thought he could add something to the rescue of Hunter and the others that no one else could.

"I can go in and get them without Lucia knowing I was there. Because of the fact that she's human now, I can simply pull the shadows around me and be in and out before she can see what I'm doing." The queen asked him about the others. "Yes, I can, and will bring them here. With the help of Vicki. She can give me the layout of the rooms where they are. That way I won't appear in the wrong place and end up with a piece of furniture in me."

"If you do this, you won't interact with her? You won't try to subdue her in any way?" He knew that Ryiah was worried about him, but he promised her that he'd just get the faeries and then leave. "If she finds you there, she will try to hurt you. I can't...I don't think I could stand it if she hurts you."

"I promise you, love, in and out and nothing more. Unless she sees me, which I'll make sure that she doesn't, then I won't have any reason whatsoever to speak to her." She asked him when he could go. "As soon as I know the rooms, I can go right after."

Vicki came to help. Davis said he'd go as well, not into the house but close enough that if he was needed, he'd be right there. Everyone agreed that the less people hanging around the house, the better it would be. Lucia might have some spies that would warn her that there were others about.

After the rooms were laid out for him, Rick willed himself to the house and pulled the darkness around him. He'd been given several cloth slings to carry the little people in. Rick decided to get the dead first, fearful that if he got Hunter first, Lucia would know something was going on. It was a risk, but he was sure that he'd be in and out before Lucia would know. Going into the house, he moved slowly to where the faeries were laying and picked them up as gently as he could. Even dead, he wanted them to have as much respect as he could give them.

After getting the other three injured ones, he took them

out to Davis. Skylar was going to come and get them as soon as he went back in for Hunter. Remy was going to come for him and the warrior to take her to Ryiah. She would be the only one who could save her.

He was standing over Hunter, having removed the glass, when he looked around the room. He wasn't going to leave anyone here that would be hurt, and nearly fell back when Hunter pointed upward. There on the ceiling were about twenty more faeries, all of them looking as terrified as he'd ever seen them. Picking up Hunter and holding her close to his body, Rick pulled open his shirt and nodded for them to come to him. In seconds he had them covered in his clothing and was ready to leave. Then Lucia came into the room.

He had no idea what he had expected in this woman. Rick knew who she was, of course. He'd seen her several times over the last few weeks. But ever since she'd been released from the cell, she'd let herself go badly. And it looked to him like some of the faeries had gotten in a few licks of their own. He held Hunter to his heart, afraid of her being hurt again, when he felt a small prick. He looked down at her and saw that she had pricked him again, but to get his attention this time.

She isn't insane. He asked her what she meant. *She is playing the fool right now in order to gain sympathy from the Gathering. She said that if they see how it has driven her mad to be without her magic, they'll return it to her. But she plans to kill them. I don't know how. And then you and Ryiah.*

Rick watched the woman and wondered why anyone would think she was anything but insane. The house was a total disaster, as well as herself. Her clothing was dirty and torn, her hair looked as if she had a large family of rats living in it, and she was talking to herself. Instead of waiting around to see what she had to say, he left. He felt Ryiah's worry and

Richard

decided that Lucia had fucked with the wrong person in this.

CHAPTER 11

Lucia looked everywhere for the fuckers. Not one of them were to be found. But what pissed her off more than anything was the fact that Hunter was gone. Not like dead gone, but simply gone. And she knew that her sister had taken her. Picking up the phone, Lucia stared at it, not having any idea how to contact her sister. The faeries were supposed to do that for her, but all they did was die. Lucia did smile about that.

Hunter had come here to tell her something. Whatever it had been had died with her. Lucia was sure that she'd killed the little thing, and she also knew that her sister would come running. But nothing had happened, not a single thing.

She'd expected her to come storming in here, demanding her friend back. Why anyone would befriend a fucking faerie like that one was beyond her. They served little purpose other than to supply someone with endless magic, as well as they were the best at keeping a house clean. Lucia missed that almost as much as she did the magic. Someone to clean up after her would have come in real handy these last few days.

Laying the phone in the cradle again, she started to go

and see to her appearance when the phone rang. Turning to stare at it, she debated whether or not to answer it when it suddenly stopped mid-ring. Turning her back on it again, she was annoyed when it rang a second time, and decided enough was enough.

Snatching up the phone, she said nothing as she listened for whatever the person on the other end had to say for herself, if anything. Just as Lucia was ready to hang up again, she heard someone say something quietly.

"What did you just say to me?" Nothing, not even a heavy breathing sound. "I don't know who this is, but I want you to stop calling here. I have better things to do than to listen to you breathing."

"I said I'm coming for you." The voice, she knew it. Not waiting for the person to say more, the receiver was nearly to the cradle when she spoke again. "Lucia, you're as good as dead as of this very moment. But I'm giving you fair warning to let you know that when you're gone, I wanted you to know it was me that put you there."

The phone went dead. The long continuous tone in her ear was both frightening and a relief. Scary because Ryiah had sounded so very serious, and relief because she knew that her sister would never harm her.

"She doesn't have it in her. No guts." As she made her way back through the house, she got down on her knees and looked for the fucking faerie. "All she ever did our whole life was cater to my needs. Do what I told her. Said what I told her to. An empty threat. There isn't any way for her to harm blood. I would hope that she'd not even try that trick on me."

Lucia was going back into the other part of the house when she saw the note on the front table. It had had a large vase on it when she'd first arrived, but the flowers in it had died and she'd taken the entire mess out back and tossed it in the pool. It had water now, she thought with a smile. Looking at the pretty handwriting on the front, she almost didn't want to open the envelope. Seeing her name in such fancy script was very nice.

"Oh bother." Opening it as carefully as she could, she laid the pretty envelope aside as she took out the single sheet of paper. It was expensive and monogramed. Across the top of the pretty paper were the initials RJ.

In the event that you don't understand what I said to you on the phone, I want to make it clear to you. When you step from your home, even to reach for a pizza that you might have brought to you, I will kill you. I am finished with you, Lucia.

Then it was signed Ryiah James.

She wanted to tear it up. Or take it to the fireplace and toss it in with the other rubbish that had been coming to her since she'd been here. Lucia even went to the living room to do so when she thought of who she was dealing with. Ryiah. Her only living relative had just threatened her.

"Well, we'll just see about that, won't we? And after all the shit I've done for her." She couldn't think of a single thing off the top of her head, but she was sure there had been something. They'd been alive for so very long that Lucia was sure that at some point she'd done something. "I cannot believe the nerve of her. First she takes my mate. Then she won't give me back my magic. And now she's threatening me. I'll show her what happens when she pulls that shit on me."

It took her all of two hours to figure out that she had to get out of the house. There wasn't anything that she could do once she was out, but since she'd been told that she couldn't leave, that was all she could think about. So of course, that was her sister's fault as well. And when she could bear it no longer, Lucia went to the door.

There were two faeries there when she stopped in the main hall.

"Fair warning, Lucia." She reminded them that she was Lady Lucia and they would use her title when they both laughed. "You are nothing. Not a single thing to us. And should Hunter not survive this, we will take great pleasure in tearing you apart."

"You? Tear me apart? Don't be stupid. You couldn't do a damned thing to me when I had my magic, and I know that you cannot do anything now. You cannot harm those with less than you." They said nothing, but she could see that they thought her stupid. "You know the rules. A faerie cannot kill or take magic from a lesser being. Every faerie knows that rule. It's the first one they teach you."

"No, the first one they teach us is to harm none. You have been harming us for decades. And now that you've hurt Hunter, we have permission to keep you in the house or we get to kill you." Lucia leapt at them, scaring the little creatures. When she laughed at them, Lucia wondered if all of them were as stupid as these were. If so, then she had nothing to worry about. They were terrified of their own shadows.

Opening the door, she let the coolness of the day wash over her. It had been a few days since she'd been out in the sunlight, and she tilted back her head to let it warm her face. This was what was so wonderful about being a faerie. The magic, for one, but the feeling that the sun gave a person when it touched their face.

She decided to go shopping. Get some cans of soup like those she'd found in the cabinets of this house and enjoyed. And then maybe she'd go to the compound and see about getting her sister to turn over her magic. It was the very least she could do after what Lucia had been through in the last few months.

Lucia took a single step, one that just put her toes over the line, when she realized that she'd made a fatal mistake. The horde had appeared out of nowhere just as the door behind her slammed closed, pushing her the rest of the way out into the opening and to certain pain. Lucia was trapped.

The magic pulled her the rest of the way out into the grass. She saw Ryiah there, her Richard standing just behind her. It occurred to her then that her sister was beautiful. Her magic, all of it, seemed to shine in a way that put a halo around the couple.

When Ryiah lifted her hand, just a simple hand to the air, the horde flew at her. Lucia tried to back into the house to get to safety, but they were too fast and the door wouldn't unlock. They were too many.

Fighting them off, she began to see that Ryiah might have been mad at her. Just for what, Lucia had no idea. As the horde tore into her, tearing at her skin, cutting through her clothing and then her flesh, she tried to find a place to hide. Anywhere but in the open. She turned to Ryiah then, and made her way there to get her to stop this nonsense.

Opening her mouth to tell Ryiah that she'd gone too far, Lucia felt them hit her body hundreds at a time. Her hair was torn from her scalp in large hanks that made blood run down her back. Even as some of it ran into her eyes she ran as quickly as she could, hoping that if she could get to Ryiah she'd see that Lucia was getting hurt. There wasn't any way that she'd let this continue otherwise.

Her mouth was full of them, and she gagged and choked as they entered her throat. The tearing of her ear from her head made her scream, which allowed more of the creatures to fill her mouth. Coughing now, she fell to the ground and was lifted up, her body dropped over and over as they tore off fingers and toes. Even as she was stripped of her clothing completely, the only barrier that she'd had between them and her, it occurred to her that they meant business, that she just might not survive this.

Her eyes were stabbed with small blades. Rubbing her hand over her head to try and stem the blood flow, she could feel the rawness where her hair had been. There was nothing there now, just pain and open wounds. Looking up when a shadow fell over her, she tried to make it out but could only see outlines. She had a feeling it was her sister.

"She died." Lucia couldn't ask her who she was talking about, but thought she might have known. That fucking faerie, Hunter. "You killed her, and now you're going to pay with your life."

Lucia reached for her, saw her arm and dropped it. The skin was gone, bone showed now, and her fingers were missing as well. Her sister had done this to her. Her own sister. When Lucia started to move, crawl from the pain, she felt something enter her mind and saw the faerie queen. With the queen's words to her, spoken softly yet loudly in her mind, Lucia felt the blade, magical and pure, enter her heart, and then she was no more.

~~~

The burial was just as Hunter would have liked…simple, with good friends and family together. Every time Ryiah thought of her friend, her only friend for so long, she hurt. Not just in her heart, but in every part of her. Ryiah sat down by the pretty faerie garden that had been built just that morning. There was even a pretty bench near it so that she could sit upon it if she wished. But for now, she sat on the ground.

176

"I have never missed anyone as I do you. You were my heart for so long that I can't think beyond that you're gone from me." Picking up one of the tiny flowers that danced prettily around the circle, she laid it in the middle. Knowing that in order for someone to disturb Hunter in her rest, they'd have to put the flower exactly where it had been before. "You'd love this garden that was made for you. Pink petals, as well as yellow blossoms that Rose brought here from her own garden. Pitch was here as well. He is so broken hearted that I sent him to his home. Whey is with him; the two of them loved you as much as I do."

Ryiah broke down then, her sobs like great painful rips in her heart that she knew would never heal. Lying down, putting her hand just near the circle, she thought of the things that the queen had told her.

"I have to choose someone to lead the army now. Yesterday I did the.... Well, yesterday I was there for them, but I don't think I can do that all the time. I need them near me, but when you were here...." She cried again and had to blow her nose twice as she tried to regain some control. "When you were here, I know that you kept them safe and together. I haven't any idea what I'm to do now. Oh Hunter, I'm so sorry that you were killed."

As she lay there, thinking of her sister now, she told Hunter what had happened. And that Lucia was no more. It was important to her that Hunter knew that. That Lucia hadn't had a proper ring made, nor had she been taken into the earth where she had died.

"The queen stabbed her with the sword of life. I'd never seen it before. It is something that you hear about for all your life, but to see it...." Ryiah wondered how many others had met their fate by being taken by the queen, and didn't want

177

to think of it. "She told me that when this is finished with the monsters from the other realms, she wishes to have a talk with Rick and me. I've not any idea what she might want, but we told her that we would. I so wish that you could be here with me when I see her. Or to see the beautiful sword. You could have—"

"Ryiah?" She looked at Rick as he sat beside her. "I've come to see if you'd join us for a meal. The faeries want you to be there when they start it."

"I've no appetite, and I've no wish to be around people just now." He nodded but didn't move away. "I have lost my best friend in the entire world because my sister was a horrible monster. Why? Why did she have to kill her, Rick? Hunter was only doing her job."

"Did I tell you that I spoke to her when I went to get her?" She sat up but didn't take her hand from the circle. "She told me where the others were, and Lucia's plans for the Gathering as well as the two of us. I think that even then she knew that you'd not be able to save her, and she wanted me to have as much information as she could get to us."

"She was such a warrior. I saw her fighting so many times, and I was forever surprised at what she was capable of. And the way that she led the others into victory was the most amazing thing." He nodded. "The others, they don't have a leader now. I don't know what to do about that."

"You should lead them." Ryiah only stared at him. "Why not? You're a faerie and they look up to you. When I saw you with them yesterday, I was amazed at how well you seemed to know what to do after telling me that you'd had no experience with them."

"I only had to tell them to go. That isn't leading them." He asked her why not. "I would have to make sure that they're trained properly. That they know what to do when they are out working. And to keep them out of trouble when there are no wars, which is most of the time. They need someone there all the time."

"And again, why not you?" He sat down beside her, and she squeaked when she was lifted up and sat on his lap. "You're brave, smart, and know a great deal more than you let on. Hunter was the best there was, but only because you were there for her. I'm sure that if given the chance, you'd be a ferocious and great leader to them. Someone that the queen could depend on as well."

"They're yours as well, the faeries." He told her that he was aware of that. "So you could lead them into war."

"I would. We'd do it together. Not to mention, they already look to you for answers." She didn't say anything. "Ryiah, you are their leader, we both are. Hiring someone else to do it, they're still going to come to you. But right now, they need you to come and be with them. They lost her as well."

"She was all I had for so long, Rick. She came to me when I was ready to just let the earth take me. She stayed with me, kept me going when there was no one else to even care about whether or not I died." He held her tighter, and she leaned into his neck. Just his scent could make her feel so much better. "What will I do now?"

"Whatever you wish, love. And know that you aren't alone any longer. You have me as well as the rest of the Brotherhood. And if this thing with Benton is finally over, I'd like to start a life. One that means we have to get up in the morning and deal with things like the cable company and bad weather. I'd also, if you would too, like to have children. As many as we can."

She looked up at him and thought of children. "You'd like

to have a baby? With me? I don't think I've ever thought....
No, I can honestly say that I've never thought of children. Not
with anyone."

He kissed her on the mouth quickly and pushed her to her
feet. When she was standing, he did as well and pulled her
into his arms. It was a wonderful feeling, having someone to
lean on, even during the good times.

"Children sound wonderful." He held her for a few
more minutes. Then she heard someone clear their throat. It
wasn't one of the Brotherhood but one of the faeries. Turning,
she wanted to tell her to go away, but knew that Whey was
worried about something.

"My lady, my lord, we would like for you to come and see
us. There are some matters that need your attention." Ryiah
turned and looked at him, and Rick still held her in his arms.
"We have many that should like to take mates. And a few
more that wish to start petitioning for the queen to allow them
to help with the newborns."

"You need me to approve you taking a mate?" She nodded
and said that most of them, because of the times, had been
living as mates, but she needed to approve their unions so that
they could go to the queen. "I don't understand why you need
me to say it's okay for you to fall in love. Isn't that something
that you just do?"

"Yes, my lady, we fall in love. A great many of us have.
But without your...I guess you could call it blessing on the
union, we aren't a couple. Then when the time comes for the
queen to pick more workers for the flowers, she only takes on
mated couples. It makes the children stronger when they are
born."

She could see that. It was the blessing part that bothered
her just a little. Who was she to say to them that they could be

in love? But nodding to Whey, she leaned back on Rick when they were alone.

"You should know that when they approached me about this a bit ago, I said they'd have to ask you as well. I'm not sure that it would be the same coming from me, but I thought it would mean more to them if we both gave our approval." Nodding, she pulled away from his body. "We're going to have to find some time to go home. I'm so hard now that I can barely move without aching to find a place to take you."

"You have to be at home to do that?" He smiled at her, and she felt her body heat up. "You look very good standing there, hard as stone, and your teeth all showing. Like a big bad wolf that might eat me."

"Oh, you can bet on that. I'm going to eat you until you're exhausted. Then I'm going to fuck you until you're unconscious." His words, spoken softly and full of need, made her wet. And when she shifted on her feet, trying to give herself a little relief, he growled low. "Let's get this taken care of so that I can take you."

"Yes, all right." She didn't move. Ryiah wasn't even sure that she could have without coming. Her body was on fire and primed for him. "I don't think we're going to make it to the blessings."

"No, we're not."

He took her into his arms and they were in the deepest part of the woods in seconds. Almost as soon as he put her back onto the ground, he was tearing her clothing off and kissing her. As he lifted her up so that she could wrap her legs around him, all she could think about was that he was going to fuck her. Now.

His hands seemed to scorch her skin. Every place that he touched her, even with his mouth, she knew that she'd bear the mark for days, if not longer. And when he bit down on her breast she came hard, screaming out for more from him even as he suckled.

"I need you." She nodded, incapable of speech at the moment. And when he dropped before her, his body as naked as hers, Ryiah held onto the branch above her head and spread her legs for him. As soon as he took her clit into his mouth, she cried out again, her body so needy that she was sure she would come several times in the next few seconds.

CHAPTER 12

Rick wanted all of her. He was sure that she'd give herself to him, in any way that he wanted. It was the deciding what part of her he wanted first that he was having trouble with.

Her breasts were full and tight, her nipples just the right size for him to take into his mouth and suckle on. Even if he wanted to bite them, which he did often, he knew that she'd hold him to her and let him have his fill.

He loved the way that her breasts filled his hands and curved just right to give way to her slim waist. The flare of her hips was full, and her ass so firm that he could hold onto her while he took her from behind. The curve of her body from her hips to her thighs made his mouth water, and he loved the way her calves seemed to be just strong enough to wrap around him, and yet not so overly muscled that she looked off balance. Ryiah had, to him, the most perfect body he'd ever seen. Even the way her neck gave way to her beautiful face was something of beauty to him.

Her scent, her taste, could bring him to his knees. Quite literally. When she moaned deep in her throat, making his cock burn with need, Rick could see stars, and oftentimes did where she was concerned.

Taking her clit into his mouth now, he savored the flavor that was unique to her, and slid his finger deep inside of her to bring her over and over for him. Rick fisted his cock with his free hand. It was either that or he was going to hurt himself. When she came for him, filling his mouth with all her juices, he felt his cock jerk in his hand and knew he was as close as he'd ever been without being deep inside of her. Standing up, he held his cock while she watched him.

"Come on me, Rick." He shook his head, pulling her to him so that he could fill her. "No, I want to feel you come on me. Spray your come all over me. Then I want you to fuck me."

When she was down on her knees in front of him, her mouth opened wide, he held onto the tree and thought about watching his cum touch her flesh. And when she licked her lips, as if readying herself for him, Rick felt like his balls exploded as streams of his cum shot from his cock.

It landed on her face, her breasts. Long streams of it touched her nipples and she rubbed it all over herself. His cock filled again as he watched her, his balls curled up to his body watching her slide her fingers into her pussy. When she came again, screaming loudly, he nearly fell forward, his body spent as he continued to fist himself.

She stood up and reached for him. He wanted to tell her that he was finished, that she'd drained him as completely as he'd ever been. But the moment that her body touched his, her cum covered breasts touching his chest, her leg running up and down his, he felt his cock harden again.

Picking her up, his mouth fused to hers, he pressed her against the tree as he slammed into her heat. As he fucked her, hard and quick, she tilted her head for him, offering up her throat for his beast. For in that moment, Rick felt him, the monster that sometimes came to him when he was hungry or afraid.

Biting into her throat, he felt her blood rush over him, through him. He drank, swallowing her life-giving blood as if it were manna for him, which he supposed in a way it was. And when he lifted his head, the blood still moving down his throat, he looked into her eyes and could see her need now, her thirst. Giving her his wrist, he put his mouth over her wound again and came as soon as she bit into him. Rick had to hold onto her or fall on his ass when his body simply gave out on him.

He held onto her for as long as he could. Rick wanted to take them to their room, lay on their bed and let his body rest. But he wasn't sure he had the energy to do that. Not so much as getting them there, but to even lift her up enough so that he could move. When she giggled, he looked down at her and rested his forehead on hers.

"You're wonderful." He grinned and even then felt the exhaustion. "You do know that I think every animal in this forest heard us. And that it'll be hours before they want to come back here again."

"Good. We have time for me to try and get my strength back. Christ, woman, you're going to kill me one of these days." Setting her down on her feet, he leaned against the tree, not letting her go. "I love you so very much. More than I ever thought possible."

"And I love you as well. While you rest up, I'm going to go and see to the faeries. I don't want them to think that we've both been eaten by some monster. Besides, if they come here and see us like this, I'm sure I'd never be able to show my face to them again."

When they were both dressed, he took her hand as they made their way to the open field. He could hear them there, all the faeries. Music was being played loudly, and he could also hear some singing going on. Rick came out from behind the trees just in time to see Remy dancing with Skylar. A dance that he was sure that Remy had learned long before anyone had marked him, and even before Skylar's great-grandparents even thought of a child being born to them.

The waltz was beautifully done by the two of them. Even as Remy held her in his arms, Rick could see how much he loved his mate. As if he were in awe of her, as well as looking like he was unsure how he'd gotten so lucky.

Rick understood that too, the way that love could make you feel like you could hold the most precious thing in the world to you, yet feel so undeserving at the same time. Pulling Ryiah to him, her body feeling as much a part of him as his own flesh and blood, he wondered what they would all do when this was finished. When they were able to go about their own lives, everyday mundane things, and not have to worry about when something or someone was going to try and kill them. He was sure the time was coming, but for him, not soon enough.

Even as he was walking toward them, his new friends, he thought of the children he might have with Ryiah. What they would be like and how they would—

The pain of the earth took him to his knees. He saw the rest of them fall as well, Remy nearly atop Skylar, the faeries taking to the skies to get away from whatever it might have been that had hurt someone so strong. The queen appeared before them, her body as racked with pain as theirs, possibly more so. Rick held his body up with everything he had, trying not to put any more pressure onto the ground beneath him. And when the queen started to sob, Rick knew as surely as he was feeling the pain again, stronger now, that they were no closer to ending this war than they had been before.

~~~

Master felt the water boil around him. Fish, dead and blackened, floated by him as he made his way to the surface. Lifting his head above the line of water, he felt the air around him. It was hot, the steam rolling around him the perfect cover for him to see what was surrounding him.

Nothing. Not a soul around, not even anything living in the waters around him. Lifting his body from the water, he stepped upon the land and felt rejuvenated. Stronger than he had before, mended in ways that he knew made him perfect. Tilting his head back, he took in a great gulp of air, feeling it fill his lungs, igniting a fire in him that he'd not felt in decades. Leaning forward again, he let out his hot breath. Fire came from his belly and blew hot flames out to the trees and land before him.

Trees burst into flames, falling to the burnt ground even as he filled his lungs again. Spraying his heat over the stone mountain, Master felt wonderful, his newfound strength gaining more rather than draining as he walked toward the mountain, burning whatever he wanted on his way.

The stone crumbled under his feet. Sand now, it gave him a little trouble, but he loved the heat of it as he smashed it under him. Walking over the still burning trees, he lifted his wings up, fanning the flames so that they would spread his fire out to more land. Master was making his mark. He had not a clue why it was so important that he do so, but he knew it was important that everyone knew that he was here.

His arm that had been useless before was strong. His

wings had been tattered and torn. They were not only whole now, but thicker, stronger than before. Lifting himself up, his wings only moving at half speed, he knew that should he want to he could fly around the world and never tire.

Master moved his tail, knocking the dead trees and stones miles from where he stood. The water behind him, covered still in a heavy mist, was dead of all life. He had no idea how he knew that, but as surely as he was standing here, he was sure he'd killed it. Roaring out his pleasure, his lungs filling again, he burned a path up the mountainside and smiled.

Whatever had happened when he'd landed in the water, whatever magic had been there, had given him life. Not just life, but had repaired him in ways that he'd never thought possible. His arm was back, his tail no longer a stump. Master was whole. Master was perfect.

Going into the cave, he burned the walls, not as much as the stone near the now dead water, but enough to warm him. He was forever cold before, but now he was near freezing. Flame was set to the stone in the middle of the room, and when they were hot, almost liquid hot, he sat down and let his mind work on what had happened.

Clearly the water had been magical. Or perhaps it had been him that was magical, and his being in it had given it and him what had been needed to heal. There was no doubt that he was completely healed. Nothing on or inside of him hurt, nor did he feel weakened by the use of his body. Master thought perhaps he could take on Rembrandt and his Brotherhood right now and come out the victor.

"They think you dead." He nodded at Ward when he spoke to him, his body dead, he knew, but talk to him he did. "They know not that you are well, and stronger. You will have the advantage this time. You can take them."

188

"And I shall." He thought of his voice and wondered at it. It was rough, strong, but sounding as if he'd been hurt somehow and had not healed properly. "Those little creatures did this to me. They were in my mouth, and I think they hurt me with their magic."

"I would say that's about right." He nodded at the invisible Ward. "Do you suppose that when you kill him, he'll have any idea that you'll be king? That you and you alone will rule the realm that he worked so hard to save?"

"I care not what he thinks so long as he is dead. And he will be now." Master lifted his arms up and flexed them. He'd never been this strong, not even when he'd started out on this mission to rule. Picking up a large stone, he crushed it with his arm that he knew had fallen off when he'd been banging around the waterways. "I should like to see him as this, between my fingers, and watch his face when I squeeze the very life from him."

"You'll do it, too. And gather the stones for you to use." He had no idea why he thought so, but Master doubted that he'd need the stones any longer. "Not for you, Benton, but for your army."

"I've no need for an army. I am an army." He stood up again, heating the walls to his cave until they began to melt. Sitting down, he knew that he'd have to be careful from now on. He'd not want to have a mountain falling upon his poor head. "I've no hunger either. Not for food or for anything else. Magic, I think it's magic that has brought me from the brink of death, and it has given me all that I need to kill him. It feels as if I have their blessing in this. Perhaps they are just as tired of Rembrandt as I."

"I like that idea. You have been given a great gift in this, and you are going to win." He nodded again at Ward. "I have spoken to Dolin and he said that he shall remain quiet for now. He does not want to tax you in talking to us both. I think, and I have thought this through very well, I believe you should rest up. Give your body a chance to grow stronger. You will need to be at your best when you take on Remy and his men."

"He has women there as well." Master thought of the women that he'd encountered when he'd been there to kill Rembrandt. "They were strong, but not like me. And I am far smarter than Rembrandt now. My mind is working out a plan even as I speak with you. I have not just become stronger. I am superior to him in all ways."

Ward agreed with him. Master thought of resting and knew that Ward was right. He wasn't going to tell him that, of course. The man was hard enough to listen to as it was. If he thought himself right, again, he would be impossible. Lying down on the warmed stones, he thought of the many ways he might kill Rembrandt. First and foremost, he was going to kill that woman.

"I shall tear her in half. Just take her body into my great claws and pull her apart. Then I might toss her away while Rembrandt begs for her life. When he is devastated, which her death will do to him, then I shall tell him that it had been my plan all along. It was to bring him to his knees over a woman. His woman." Ward told him he was most brilliant. "I am. I have said this to you before."

"So you have, so you have." Master closed his eyes, thinking of his plans and how he was going to make them happen. "You will need to get more of the stones. An army, like the one that drove you to the water, will need to be put together."

"Nay, I have told you, I've no need for an army. I will take them on myself and win." He knew that he could and didn't like that Ward kept insisting that he was going to need help. "If you do not stop in this army business, I shall not speak to you again. I have more power than I have ever had. And there is no reason for me to think that the earth will not come to my aid should I need it. Rembrandt will be dead soon and I will rule all."

But he would have an army. Those little creatures that had attacked him, they would be his. He would have to rule them harshly; they did try to kill him after all. But without their help, he might not have ever figured out that the water was what he'd needed and that the earth was his ally in this. She would help him like none other. And if she did not, then he would destroy her as well. Master was going to rule and the earth was going to have to learn who was boss.

"When do you think to go after him?" He had no idea and said as much to Ward. "I think you should wait, for a bit anyway. Give them time to be caught off guard. Make them lazy in their thinking that you shan't return."

"But I shall return and they will know my wrath." Ward told him that they'd be nothing but dust under his feet when he was finished. "Yes, dust. I shall enjoy that. Much more than I thought possible."

He felt his body begin to relax. He was suddenly very tired and wanted to be at his best when it was time to see to Rembrandt. Master knew that he'd have to get used to his newfound strength. To learn to fly again, to use his tail. It had been a very long time since he'd been able to do much more than to run away and hide. He would hide no more. Master was going to be a force that would take over this world, and everyone would know when he was about.

"Do you suppose that I can become human again?" Ward asked him what he meant. "You know, become my other self?

191

I think it would be easier to come and go when I find myself a home suitable for a king. Master of all that he sees."

"You will need a crown too. It is a shame that you destroyed the one that Dolin had made so long ago. It would have looked very good sitting upon your head. You will need a throne as well, somewhere to sit so that you can look down upon your subjects." He was liking this plan more and more. "Yes, you will be a master in not just name but in reality soon. And I shall be there for you, telling you what to do."

Master was just drifting off to sleep when he realized what Ward had said to him. No one was going to tell him what to do. When he was finished with this thing with Rembrandt, Ward and Dolin were going to have to leave him alone. And if Mary even tried to talk to him, he was going to take care of her as well. He had not one clue as to how he was going to do that, but soon. He'd have to cut them out of his life soon.

Master was going to need no one when Rembrandt was gone. He was going to rule and there would be no stopping him from doing so.

NOW AVAILABLE IN THE
BLOOD BROTHERHOOD SERIES

COMING SOON

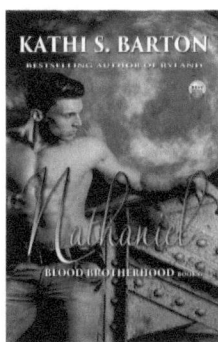

Paranormal Romance with a Bite!
Blood, Body and Mind:
A Paranormal Romance by Kathi S. Barton

Your FREE Copy is Waiting...

Aaron MacManus, the new master vampire of the realm just wanted to go out and meet some of his subjects and to figure out what needed to be done to set things right.

April and Demetrius Carlovetti own an air service and are the most trusted and well liked vampires in Aaron's realm. What he didn't expect when he visited them was betrayal. His own bodyguards try to murder him and blame it on the Carlovetti's.

Sara Temple was not a vampire. She pilots planes for the Carlovetti Airways. She had secretes of her own and working for this small air service is keeping her out of sight. The last thing she wanted to do was save a vampire, even an extremely good looking one.

Sera was only trying to survive but with Aaron she becomes embroiled in politics, the magic of several realms involving a queen in peril, magical beings, passion and love.

Blood, Body and Mind, the first book in the Aaron's Kiss series.

http://eepurl.com/brCBvP

Join my Readers' Group and get a copy
of Blood, Body and Mind FREE

http://eepurl.com/brCBvP

Before You Go...

HELP AN AUTHOR

write a review

THANK YOU!

Share your voice and help guide other readers to these wonderful books. Even if it's only a line or two your reviews help readers discover the author's books so they can continue creating stories that you'll love. Login to your favorite retailer and leave a review. Thank you.

AWARD WINNING, BESTSELLING AUTHOR

Kathi Barton, author of the bestselling series Force of Nature, lives in Nashport, Ohio with her husband Paul. In addition to writing full time Kathi likes to spend time with her eight grandkids, three children and three children-in-laws. She writes to relax and have fun.

Her muse, a cross between Jimmy Stewart and Hugh Jackman brings them to life for her readers in a way that has them coming back time and again for more. Her favorite genre is paranormal romance with a great deal of spice. You can visit Kathi on line and drop her an email if you'd like. She loves hearing from her fans. aaronskiss@gmail.com.

Follow Kathi on her blog: http://kathisbartonauthor.blogspot.com/

www.ingramcontent.com/pod-product-compliance
Lightning Source LLC
Chambersburg PA
CBHW032134170626
46808CB00006B/2228